I0682925

# GOLD MAN REVIEW

# ISSUE 12

Gold Man Review is published annually by Gold Man Publishing.

The editors invite submissions of previously unpublished works of fiction, nonfiction, and poetry. Manuscripts can be submitted at www.goldmanpublishing.com by following our submission guidelines.

Copyright 2022/2023 Gold Man Publishing / Gold Man Review
9730 Flourish Drive
Redding, CA 96001
ISBN: 979-8-9870253-0-7

No part of this work may be reproduced or transmitted in any form or by any means, electronic or mechanical, including but not limited to photocopying and recording, or by any other information storage or retrieval system without proper written permission of the publisher.

Address all requests to:
Heather Cuthbertson
Editor-in-Chief
Heather.Cuthbertson@GoldManPublishing.com

# Contents

# POETRY

# NONFICTION

# Issue 12 Editor's Letter

This is going to be a short letter.

I was really, really tempted to leave the Editor's Letter at just that one sentence. I thought it would be funny and reflective of the kind of year we've had. And what a year! I think I say that every letter, but lately it feels like I open my eyes on a Monday morning and next thing I know, it's Sunday. It's a little like being on a human hamster wheel.

Gold Man has been busy too, as always, both with compiling this year's issue and also getting through the year together. In 2022, every single one of the editors moved. Two went to brand new towns and states, making for some hard goodbyes. The other two, myself included, moved to a new house, but in the same town. It might have just been up a street, versus three hours away or 27 hours away, but still, a move's a move. You have to pack everything. Go through junk drawers. Get rid of all the things you haven't looked at for years, find the things you've forgotten for years. Moving is a process of both purging and rediscovery, a tally of one's life by the things that surround us, most while we are unaware. With all the editorial changes, I don't know what it'll be like moving into our Lucky Number 13 Issue, but I know it won't be the same. Twelve years of Gold Man Review has showed me that the only thing I can count on is the shuffle.

You might notice we gave Gold Man itself a little shake up. If you've been following us for the last decade, you'll notice that in this issue we've clumped the work into groups: Fiction, Poetry, and Nonfiction, instead of having them blend together. Pretty easy peasy, but it made sense to do it this way. Every year we send our issue to the Best of Anthologies and other prize anthologies and figured this method would make it easier for those editors to find our contributors' work, especially since most are genre-specific. We added some fun little activities before each section because, you know, why not? After 12 years, we can do what we want around here.

For anyone interested in submitting to Gold Man Review in 2023, I thought I would talk about what we're looking for in submissions and what we're not looking for. For nonfiction, it goes without saying that we're always hungry for great nonfiction. Who isn't? It's notoriously hard to find and it's the least amount we receive every year. Where are all the nonfiction writers? I love fiction, but, seriously, isn't truth supposed to be stranger than fiction? It's what they say, right? When we do receive nonfiction, we're looking primarily for memoir pieces. You can talk about anything that interests you but have *you* in it somewhere.

For fiction, one surefire way to get our interest is to keep the story on the shorter side. It's not a guaranteed acceptance, but it will get you read faster. You might notice that most of our fiction this year is short. It's not a coincidence. Anything longer than 10 pages must be absolutely freaking phenomenal to keep us reading. Most just aren't and half the feedback on those submissions is that "it could have been cut some." If it's in our journal and it *is* longer, then it's a huge indicator to PLEASE READ IT (including nonfiction). As far as fictional content, we like the interesting, the random, the strange, and the bizarre. For instance, there's the guy who comes to realize something about himself by how his wife puts the coffee cups away and then there's the guy who does the same but it's not coffee cups, it's his wife's collection of department store mannequins she keeps in their bedroom. It's the everyday thrown off kilter: that's our jam.

As far as poetry, the same rules apply as fiction. We're not the best place for nature or medical trauma poems. I know we've published them in the past, but we're more drawn to poetry that matches our fiction tastes, to be honest, and those are the ones we gravitate towards.

I know I meant for this letter to be short and here I am rambling while I have boxes to unpack. We hope you enjoy the pieces we selected this year. We are very proud of our contributors' work and think they are amazing. This was a fun issue to put together, although it's also been a little bittersweet since we'll be missing some faces around the table in 2023. But in the words of LMFAO, every day I'm shuffling.

Now off for Lucky Number 13.

*Heather Cuthbertson*
Editor-in-Chief
Gold Man Review

# Gold Man Review Editors
# Issue 12

Heather Cuthbertson
Editor-in-Chief

Nicklas Roetto
Project Editor

Daniel Link
Editor

Ashley Rich
Editor

Eric Halpenny
Editor
Chef Extraordinaire

# GOLD LIBS FICTION STYLE

## Legend of the Lengendary Fiction
### (use titles to play)

Basil Mint Ice Cream
Deathbed Catholic
Everybody Wants to be a Papa
Forever Racing

Singapore
The Art of Loving
The Koudelka Exhibit

Sometimes writing is torture. It makes us feel like a _____.
It makes us beg for the end, but terrified of reaching it. We feel like
we are _____ toward a finish line that is always too far away
and just out of reach. Is it still fun? Yes. Do we keep coming back for
more? We do. And why? Because _____.

The words that pour from our fingertips are like air to our reader's
lungs. Like _____ to a parched, aching throat. Words are what
drive us, and what our reader's need.

The blank page is a king cobra dancing in the streets of _____.
We see it, and we must tame it. And we can't do that unless all demands are met. We need a cold drink on the table and our favorite
white noise humming in the background and every speck of dust
vanquished from the baseboards. Then, and only then, can we finally
write.

Sometimes sentences appear on the page slower than turtles through
peanut butter, but progress is progress. It doesn't matter if it takes
hours, weeks, months or even years to finish a project. We bend letters and edit them into deeper meanings. Our words are more than
stories. They are prized treasures to display at the _____, for
all to see!

Readers only see the finished product. They don't know the tears
that stained the pages. They see our stories, and once they leave our
hands, do they still belong to us? No. They belong to them, our readers, and that's why we write. It's the purest _____.

Provided by Editor, Ashley Rich

# Jalapeño Cilantro Rice

## Provided by Editor, Eric Halpenny
## (his own recipe)

### Ingredients

2 jalapeños roughly chopped
1 bunch of cilantro roughly chopped
1/2 cup of chicken broth

2 cups rice
1/2 cups diced onion
2 cloves of garlic chopped
1 cup of sweet corn
3 1/2 cups chicken broth
2 tbsp cooking oil

### Directions

1. Blend jalapeños, cilantro, 1/2 cup chicken broth until smooth (you can roast the jalapeños for a few minutes in a pan to darken the skin a little for added flavor)
2. Warm cooking oil over medium high heat in a large frying pan with high sides. Add rice and sauté for a few minutes until some grains start to brown
3. Make a well in the center of the rice to expose the pan and add onions and garlic. Cook for about 1-2 minutes, keeping the onions moving to prevent scorching.
4. Add chicken broth and jalapeño mixture and bring to a simmer
5. Reduce heat if needed to prevent boiling, and simmer until rice is tender and liquid is absorbed. If liquid absorbs too quickly, add chicken broth or cold water.
6. After rice is tender, add corn and stir. You can reserve some chopped cilantro and add with corn at this point if desired.

# Everyone Wants to be a Papa
## daniel o'leary

When she turned thirty, she threw herself a Roaring Twenties party because she considered herself part of another lost generation and thought herself a little clever. Thirty of her closest friends were invited to her downtown Oakland apartment for an evening of enforced, strict, Parisian-themed fun. Her friends were mostly white, creative, and mostly smart, so all the painters were in attendance: Picasso, Matisse, Dali, and even Severni since he was so easy with his monocle and bowler. A husband and wife came dressed as Mr. and Mrs. James Joyce–gender swapped, of course.

The two Hemingways arrived, recognized each other, and cut to the kitchen. One wore a heavy woolen sweater and thick mittens, a pint of schnapps poking out from his back pocket. The other wore old-fashioned fishing gear and placed two chilled bottles of Spanish white on the kitchen counter before picking up a pre-filled glass of champagne.

"Some beautiful flies you have there, Hem," Ernest said pointing with his mitten to the hooks on the fishing vest. "Handmade?"

"The best flies are hand-tied," Hem said finishing his champagne. "How about some of that liquor there, Ernest?"

Ernest handed the flat bottle over. "The Austrians I ski with in the high mountain passes make their schnapps from wild raspberries. This is some German production."

"It cuts damn fine, still," Hem said. "It speaks more to the cold though. On hot evenings, even the false heat of all these strangers pressed together in this apartment, there is nothing for the head like cold wine." Hem grabbed a bottle of the Spanish white. "Take a slug of that."

Ernest drank a gulp, then another.

"That chills the teeth roots. Would be fine for a day at the tracks."

"Tomorrow," Hem said. "We'll go play the horses at Golden Gate Fields."

"Is the track grass or dirt?"

"They have both," Hem replied. "I know a jockey who races there – Fernandez. Such courage you've never seen for such a small man."

Hem was cut short by a shout from the entryway. A man sporting a beard–dyed Andalusian-gray–swung a bottle of Havana Club into the room.

"Cuba Libres in the kitchen!" Papa shouted.

"That's not Twenties Paris," the hostess of the party said as Papa swaggered around her.

"Paris is not yours; Paris is not mine. The Parisians don't even have Paris," Papa said. "Paris is washed into the Seine each morning and Paris falls from the linden trees every autumn."

The hostess stared at Papa with her mouth slightly open.

"Swell birthday party," Papa said as he leaned in and pecked her on the cheek. He turned and saw Hem and Ernest standing there in the kitchen.

"Gentlemen," Papa said. "Fine night for a drunk."

"Too right."

"We'll be getting there presently."

"Be a champ and mix us up some cocktails," Papa said, handing the rum to Ernest. Papa fished a lime from his shirt pocket and tossed it to Hem. "Cut this up, chap."

"What do we look like, barmen?" Ernest asked.

"Barman is an honorable line," Papa said sticking his fingers through his belt loops. "I've put more trust in barmen than I have my wives."

"I don't cut fruit," Hem said quickly. "You work for a man once and he owns you for the rest of your years."

"I was asking for a favor, my boy, no need to push philosophy around the room like some poor European," Papa said. "All bluster and bosh."

"I'll give you bosh."

"You want a bit of a row?" Papa asked smiling. "Fine night for a row!"

Papa and Hem began grappling, knocking small ceramic plates to the ground.

"Now boys, knock it off with all this rubbish," Ernest said, grabbing Hem from behind. Hem freed an arm from Papa's grasp and launched an elbow into Ernest's face.

"Christ, man!" Ernest shouted. He tangled Hem in a headlock and tugged him backwards. Hem flailed and sent a charcuterie board flipping through the air.

Papa screamed out a laugh and tore off his shirt, exposing a round-ed-out belly. "Let him go. I want a fair fight, here," Papa said as he popped a soft jab at Ernest's nose.

"Papa I was trying to help you!" Ernest said, releasing Hem.

"A man helps himself to the top," Papa said. "An Italian moun-taineer told me that."

It was a blithe fight, punchy and wild.

"You strike like a woman with your small hands," Hem said hoarsely into Papa's ear.

"Women are fearless. You would know that if you ever loved one," Papa said, throwing a wild haymaker.

Off to the side, Ernest was stuffing torn napkin into his bleeding nose. He tipped the last gulp of wine out of a bottle and spiked the bottle against the floor. He charged. With his chest, he caught Papa and Hem in a tackle and the three of them plunged through a wood-en side table. All of them were laughing, shouting now, as they rolled across the original hardwood floor.

"This is how they celebrate a successful hunt in the Kenyan high-lands!"

"I saw a Chippewa initiation ritual like this!"

"You boys have never seen a true English donnybrook, it seems!"

"I called the cops!" the hostess screamed from behind the couch. The other guests were streaming out the front door. Two men—one black and one white—pushed against the flow and entered the apart-ment. They both had on shorts and boxing gloves and wore matching boxing robes. They ran over and began raining hammer fists onto the other three Hemingways.

"What's this fresh hell?" Hem cried covering his head and neck.

"I won't suffer this," Ernest said as he swept the legs out from un-der the black Hemingway.

Soon both boxing Hemingways had been torn down into the writhing mass of elbows and fists. The hostess sprinted for the door and took one final look back at the devastation in her apartment.

"You better be running out for ice!" Papa screamed after her.

The slamming front door brought pause to the frenzy. Slowly, they released each other and came to their feet.

The white boxing Hemingway cracked his neck and asked, "Fun party?"

"Pretty drab affair until you lot showed up," Hem said. He pulled one of the fish hooks out of his forearm and swore.

The black pugilist Hemingway asked, "Is there anything to drink or should we send for a bottle?"

They all laughed and moved into the kitchen. Hem uncorked his last bottle of white and they passed it around the circle, quickly finishing it.

"My boyfriend here said I should go as Langston Hughes. Just cause I'm black I can't be Hem. I have to be Hughes. Or Du Bois."

"Oh my god, this again. I was up all night sewing these precious robes and he can't get past the whole Hughes thing."

"Fellas," Papa said. "We can fight after we get proper liquored. Let's make for a bar."

So, bullying each other, they made for a bar. Papa checked that the front door was locked before they set off into the night, all still Hemingway but for none of the reasons they thought.

# Singapore
## michael pearce

You step into air that makes your skin itch. Down the boarding stairs and onto the tarmac in this little airport, your first taste of weather in your hometown in how long? Was it always so dry here, the light so well mannered, the clouds so insubstantial? Your throat seems confused about what direction it's swallowing in.

Tom is waiting just past the security gate. He greets you with that old conspiratorial look, but you both know the game has changed. He's no longer that outlaw kid who owned nothing but a pool cue and an old BSA motorcycle, who smoked too much weed and never stayed anywhere longer than a couple days.

You notice a woman standing to his right and a step back and realize it's her, Allison—he's mentioned her every so often. You met her once: she sat on the back of the BSA with her hands in Tom's front pockets, looking wasted, just one more in the string of women he partied with and moved on. "Well, hi there," she says, not quite smiling. They're engaged.

She looks you over and suddenly you see yourself through her green eyes, see a guy who dresses and talks a bit out of sync. Then again, maybe she sees an adversary, somebody who just arrived not from another country but from Tom's past, a place she can never go, can never share with Tom. You decide that her greeting to you was shrunken and hard, like dread, or worse.

And Tom. He seems his old self… plus the big new house and the thriving business with its thirty-odd employees, satellite souls who need him to put food on their tables and self-respect in their spines. The three of you stand at the luggage carousel as bags that look like yours glide by. He says, "How was the flight?" but he means something bigger, more abstract, and you have no answer, so you say "Oh, uneventful." But he holds his gaze: the ball is still in your court.

"In the Singapore zoo," you say, "there are three white tigers. Last week a man climbed into their enclosure—they tore him to pieces."

"I can't believe it," Tom says, "that happened here, some California zoo. A guy was taunting this tiger and it jumped the fence and killed him."

"Jesus," you say, and you both marvel at the universality of human idiocy. You could go on—that tiger is a stand-in for nature, death, time, evolution, the revolt of the colonized class—but what's the point? Such deliberations are part of a camaraderie that feels remote, shaky.

Allison looks annoyed. "This is how brothers re-bond?" She looks around, as though a fourth person might join the group. "Well, so. Did you have a girlfriend there?"

"Yeah, kind of. Not really." The words are so vague that you know she sees through them, sees the chaos in your eyes. That look of hers pushes you back across an ocean and into a place that still breathes—voices echo in the bars and offices and commuter trains, and the air is not the nothing you're standing in now. It's thick and sweet and close as a blanket. Your memory navigates like a drone to Fann's apartment, you are hovering there with her oddly colored furniture, her alien, hybrid accent, her nephew's pet lizard. Your mind's ear fills with her breathing in the night, the same pitch and timbre as the air condition-er. A body, a culture that you couldn't fully embrace, yet so vivid they obscure older memories of your life here.

"I mean yeah, I had a girlfriend. It didn't work out." You recognize the shade of green in Allison's irises: Robin Hood's hat. "I wish I knew why."

Her gaze softens. A knowledge that you've been walking around with, though you've managed to hold it at the edge of awareness, leans in close. It wasn't Fann, or Singapore, or the job, it was you, who you were becoming, that kept you outside of... of what?

You arrived there with what looked like a good job teaching English. It took two years to figure out that you'd never get anywhere near the pay and benefits they'd promised. By then you'd been hanging out at the Sentosa Casino, depressed, barely holding onto enough of your paycheck to eat and pay rent, floating through refrigerated air trying to look amused and in control. You abandoned your rented studio, moved your stuff over to Fann's. Then, one fateful binge of a night, you lost it all at roulette. The floor manager, Darren, liked you, figured your military background would be an asset to his security team. He hired you with a contract that said you would not gamble at Sentosa.

You began another new life, walking the rainbow swirl of that vast carpet, observing tourists with a sad disdain. You often slept there, in a basement room, saw less and less of Fann. You saved money. Sometimes you'd phone Tom, each call a receding snapshot, smaller, fainter.

Now this man in front of you is trying to connect with his blurry, troubled older brother. "So," he smiles, "the room is ready. Over the garage. You'll like it." Maybe he gets it, how far you've traveled, drifted, fled. Yes, he's become something of a stranger. But he's your link. Your parents retired, moved to one of those little states in the upper right corner, near Canada. Your old neighbor, Hal, texted a year ago that he'd decided to keep Frankie, your dog. If you visit them, Frankie will surely growl.

The room above Tom's garage will be your outpost, your private immigration island. Tom and Allison will indulge you until you get back on your feet, help you assimilate into your homeland. Returning is not an event, it's an undertaking. You are somewhere old, familiar, and utterly foreign.

# The Art of Loving

## ash witherell

We drove to Venice Beach, and along the road were billboards. The Hollywood-made girls had fat lips and thin noses and rich dark eyeshadow, and we envied them and picked favorites to crush on.

Hollywood hadn't made us, so we made ourselves. We had coconut curls and sunscreen faces and we dressed in bikinis and band t-shirts and oversized jeans with the pockets hanging out. May pierced her nose and Kiara wore headscarves in shades of red and purple and sometimes she'd take them out going down the highway and her black hair would be a mess for three days.

"Why'd y'all let me do that?" she'd demand. "Stupid."

Kiara didn't stand out in a crowd but when she smiled it was the prettiest thing you'd ever seen. Her face was smooth and round, and she hated it. She wanted a thin little jaw and a thin little nose like Anya Taylor-Joy.

Later on, she got a nose job and straightened it out so her eyes glittered. May said she did it for the boys, but the boys didn't notice if she had a round nose or a straight one. They looked at her baggy jeans and bikini top and bright white smile and knew what they wanted.

Boys wanted us a lot. They drifted in and out of our lives: Angel with the spiked hair and the beach net; Hiram, who was skinny and dark and spoke in one tumbling waterfall; Case from San Diego, who May stayed with six months before she found some inland girl with brown hair and a scholarship to Pepperdine in the bed. Pepperdine girl baked May a chocolate pound cake in apology, and they talked about evil, unfaithful men who didn't deserve a dime of what they gave them, and after that Pepperdine girl— whose name we never knew— came by once a week to watch Great British Bake Off and smoke weed on May's back patio.

We all had Pepperdine girls. Mine was a dark-haired lifeguard who spoke Spanish. The warm syllables floated out of his mouth like summer sun. He loved banana pancakes and cheap paperbacks, and he ran fingers through my hair and called me *cielo*.

I told Kiara I loved him. She laughed and shook her head, and all at once I knew I didn't.

A month later, I lent my lifeguard fifty bucks for a Greyhound toward Vegas. He kissed me goodbye and left to drive taxis. I never saw him again.

It wasn't a betrayal. It was a moving on.

Nothing's stationary in California. The ground shakes and the fashions come and go like wildfire and the strip malls build up and tear down again. What's in one day goes out the next, Kiara in particular. One day she'd be in vintage jumpsuits like Rosie the Riveter— the next decked out in gold chains and baggy t-shirts— then formal, in a baby blue suit found in the back of Goodwill.

"I play to type," she said, and she did.

May was a free spirit in her own way. Her words were wicked. She was prickly like cacti.

"Kiara looks damn fine," I said to her once. We were in the back of her minivan, doors open, laid out on towels with the beach out in front of us and Chinese takeout on our laps.

"She'd better," May said.

May had a way of knowing. She was half-Chinese and LA-born. I was inbred with Midwestern whiteness, a sort of malevolent-benevolence I was trying to shake, a hole where a heart should be.

"May," I said.

"Yeah?"

"I think I love you."

May went quiet and appraised me. She had dark eyes and oil-slick makeup, and her skin was as gold as the beach.

She took another bite of takeout.

"Sweetheart," she said, "don't put that on me."

I couldn't.

We went back to chewing. Down at the shore, Kiara tumbled in the surf.

Home that week was painful. Normally, when the arthritis hit, I dragged May or Kiara out and partied it back into a black hole, popping ibuprofen in the bathroom, rubbing diclofenac into my swollen hands and feet. I didn't need to drink— I got high off my friends, the glitter in eyeshadow and the scent of shampoo in hair.

That week May got sick of me, and Kiara said she was visiting her aunt in New Orleans. I sprayed perfume on my wrist and sniffed it like a socialite doing cocaine. I tried to dance but my feet rebelled against the silence, the straps, the heels. I baked a chocolate cake and threw it up into the sink. My apartment was quiet: Iowa-quiet, like the morning after. It felt cold and empty and blank.

I hadn't been able to stand those stiff-still mornings, dew on the grass, zipping into dresses for church. I loathed the small talk and the tight shoes and most of all the whispering. My Mom whispering, the scent of her.

"Quick and quiet," she would say. "Today's not for you."

I ran away from Iowa when I turned eighteen and I bought the clothes in shop windows and wore deep purple lipstick and got good at rolling my hips and doing liner so my eyes turned up instead of down. I didn't regret a moment of it, even the ones that hurt me. They scrubbed my soul raw like a beach-tumbled stone. They made me feel like I had a name, a life, a heart, a being. Iowa made me feel like nothing at all.

Whiteness was a dead thing floating in water.

It stole so much of me.

I think maybe I was born without a soul and spent my whole life trying to find it. I found my way to California where there were Chinese immigrants and Afro-Latinas and I tried to fill myself up with them, my colorful people, the way they laughed and danced and made the air glow. I felt like the way things were, nothing ever really went away. Plantations were alive in prison cells. Sometimes I was holding the whip. It was a whirlwind of blame and predation and trying to be good, answering the unanswerable.

I tried to atone for a past piled with bodies whose bones still lie in apartment buildings and sewer drains. Apologies fell on dead air 'cause dead don't answer.

I dug my fingernails into friends and fed off them.

I was sick of feeding.

Dressed in my worst wool-knit sweater, I stepped out of the apartment and hobbled my way towards the church.

"Stupid," Kiara would say. "What's there for you?"

I wasn't sure.

I still went to service when I felt down. I didn't go for the preaching or the wine or the body of Christ. I went for the anonymity of a woman in church.

I went for the stained-glass windows.

I walked down the pavement and kept my eyes on the gum on the sidewalk.

Halfway down the road I saw a girl smoking outside an apartment building and realized it was Kiara, and I ducked behind a dumpster to clutch my knees to my chest like I was five years old. A few minutes later she came walking past me and May came after her and they both stopped at the light and laughed and teased and kissed just like that. It wasn't a big kiss, all romantic-type. It was the way people kiss to get going. The light turned and they stepped out in the crosswalk— Kiara's dress shining, May's long hair down behind her— and swerved to the left and were gone.

I stayed behind that dumpster until my knees ached. When the cold got bad, I got up and went to the bar and drank too much and played the virgin and batted my eyes at the frat boys down the way, hooking up until I couldn't feel a thing besides hands on mine, lips on lips, heat and sweat and the way the light shone off the windowpane.

That night I dreamed about my mom. She was putting lipstick on in the mirror. She never wore lipstick.

There's something I try to hide: I'm a bad woman. I love my mom to death. I spent my whole childhood trying to get some speck of warmth out of her.

The night before I left Iowa, my mom took me shopping for the first time.

"A girl isn't anything unless she's pretty," she'd said. "Not anything, these days."

We stood in Macy's and perused the rows and rows of blouses and dyed jeans. Mom had a scowl on her face and a drab gray sweater on her shoulder. I looked at lace bras and thought about girls on camera.

Mom eyed me, and I turned my head away.

"You listen to me," she said. "I was pretty once."

I was desperate to do something. I wanted to scream, yell, cut my hair off. I wanted shots and edibles and cocaine and a man in the back room.

"Then," Mom said, "I had you."

Had me: yes, she'd had me. She'd wrapped herself around, possessed my body for twenty-two years. It was her way of loving.

Later I'd get tattoos on my hip, my breast, my thigh; the biggest was a snake winding 'round my crotch, its head resting on my stomach. To me, it always had my mother's name.

She was my original sin— the source of it. Every man I found was her. Every touch of fingernails was her hand on my hair. She'd ruined me.

Kiara found out and her face wrapped up in sympathy.

"That's fucked," she said. "You know that, right?"

I did. I didn't.

It was what I knew of love.

I opened my eyes the morning after. I'd drank until I blacked out. I felt makeup on my face, the pounding of a hangover, the slick of a hookup.

"Headache?" a voice asked.

I opened my eyes and blinked. The face next to mine slid into focus. It was May.

She pushed something at me, and I took it: a glass of water.

"Alka-Seltzer," May said, leaning back on the pillows. Sheets shifted against skin, and her long hair tangled in the curves of rumpled bedding.

I took a sip. It was cool.

We sat in silence for a moment, May's stare heavy on my shoulders.

She spoke before I did.

"You called us last night," she said.

I looked down at the sheets.

May sighed and sunk down further, wrapping her legs in the white cloth. "You were going on about going home."

I opened my mouth and shut it again.

May closed her eyes. I curled into myself, waiting.

"You belong here," she continued. "Maybe not forever. Maybe just another day."

I knew then we weren't in love and never would be.

The birds sang outside the window, soft, lilting.

"You're an idiot," May said.

I leaned my head against her shoulder. Down below I heard the door open. It was Kiara with the morning groceries, coming home.

After I ran away from Iowa, everyone told me how sorry they were. They spoke my mother's name in hisses. May took me out to lunch and hugged me at the end. I buried my secret deep.

The secret was I loved her— the secret was I'd liked it.

The secret was I take what love I can get.

# The Koudelka Exhibit

## william hawkins

When Benton called, I was on the patio, low in a lounge chair, my hand in a book of short stories, my eye on a houseleek petal blooming out a tin pot. He asked if I wanted to go with him to the Getty to see the Koudelka exhibit, and maybe dinner after, maybe drinks. Then he said the word maybe without anything but breath behind it. I told him I would love to and spent the next twenty minutes dressing myself before he pulled up in the driveway and honked his horn twice to let me know.

"Alyssa is crazy, right?" he asked as hello. "Absolutely crazy. All we do is fight. That's all we do. I get home from work, we fight. We go out to dinner, we fight. Isn't that crazy? Do you know what she wants us to do? She wants us to go to the desert for a week. A week! Without anything. Like, cell phones or computers or, like, anything. A week! Just us. She says, 'We need to find out who we are together.' Isn't that crazy?"

I offered monosyllabic affirmations of his words and otherwise let him talk. And he did, all the way up the 405, one more in the artery of taillights pumping its way into the Santa Monica Mountains. We talked about Alyssa and Benton's job and nothing else in particular.

Once we were free of the 405, we parked on the second level of the Getty's garage, joining a group of Buddhist monks in the elevator to the tram. The monks were either talking about something important or inconsequential in a foreign language. They wore neon orange vestments and had the eagerness of men not looking ahead. We were in front of them in the line to the tram. In front of us, a herd of teenagers in grey jumpsuits with the words 'Tianjin Number One High School' printed on the back in blocks of English characters.

"I've never been to the Getty," Benton said as we filed aboard the tram, "can you believe it? Isn't that insane? I've lived here for six years. Never been. Then I start thinking about all the things I haven't done, and I go crazy. Do you ever do that? I mean, do you ever just sit down and figure out all the things you haven't done yet? Dude. It's depressing."

The tram was slow. Benton stopped talking, maybe to come up with more things he hadn't done. I listened to a man next to me tell his friend about a woman he met in Paris and her family vacation home on Lake Geneva. It sounded lovely. But before the story could reach its tragic ending—why else would he be here, if the ending wasn't tragic?—the tram stopped, and we made our mob way up the sandstone steps of the museum.

The Getty is reminiscent of nothing if not a fortress on a hill, a fortification against all the Los Angeles below, all white stone and ceramic and glass, hollow spaces swollen with the echoes of people passing through. Benton and I followed each other into the nearest pavilion, passing a sign which explained why Germanic glassware and illuminated manuscripts were important. We didn't read it. The walls of that first room were lined with stained glass, lifted in metal frames, lead strips woven through the silicon portraits, binding the hands and faces of pilgrims and sinners, crisscrossing their bodies, making people out of pieces while all the saints gazed down beneficently, clear of any lead, their faces whole, features made of soft white light, banners over-head proclaiming their life in Latin. There was Saint Margaret, there was Saint Catherine, there was the Madonna and her mother and her Son, holy things of corrupted glass.

Benton said, "Pretty."

In the next rooms were displays of medieval glassware, ornamental pots and pans. There was a wall devoted to pilgrim flasks, shaped like water-bearing gourds of desert nomads, each one increasingly ostenta-tious. In the center of one—made of, as best I could tell, a dull-gleam-ing copper—a scene was painted of a figure tied to a tree on a hill, looking to the city below, the face rendered in short flat strokes. I read the placard below it. It said:

*The figure depicted is bound to a tree. This image, popular in Italy in the 1500s, is an allegory of love, shown as a bittersweet force that holds its victim captive. In keeping with this theme, the central scene is encircled by a rope.*

It was true; the border between the painted scene and the rest of the flask was a rough hemp rope, one big noose. One of the students from Tianjin Number One High School stepped beside me and took a picture with his phone, then shuffled to the next exhibit, took another picture, and moved on. They were all doing it, all these high schoolers in their grey jumpsuits and white sneakers, taking pictures with their phones, practically running through the rooms. I wasn't sure if it was a tourist thing, a teenager thing, or some strange intersection of the two.

"Probably a project," Benton said. "Seems a shame to come seven thousand odd miles just to take pictures of things you can already find on the Internet." He laughed and brushed his arm against mine as he moved forward. "People are funny."

In the illuminated manuscript room, there were pedestals of choir books with stenciled flowers in the margins, of such precision that, even when I bent down until my nose nearly touched the glass display, I couldn't make out where the ink ended. Gold dust glittered deep in Gothic petals, shaped in constellations too small for naked eyes. Beside me there was a woman, blond, in a pink-and-white striped tank top. She was at least fifty years old. Her skin was the worn-down color of a pine bartop. She was with a man. He was at least seventy. He had a full head of hair, tied back into a ponytail. He had his hand on her ass. When he was done looking at the manuscript, he pushed the hand on the ass forward.

"Letch," Benton called him.

We followed the old man and his lover upstairs to the paintings, room after open room of oil on canvas, saints and sinners, Christs and Virgin Marys, Biblical landscapes, Greek myths and pastoral scenes, painted in pigments scratched from the surface of the earth and bled from flowers and herbs, square worlds made between contrast and harmony. We walked, Benton and I, under the gentle gazes of thirty-seven Madonnas. The back of our necks prickled in the aim of twenty-three drawn bows of Cupid, themselves under the watchful eyes of at least a hundred puttos. Around us the crowd moved like cream in a forgotten cup of coffee, shifting, breaking apart, wobbling in place, some inspecting the paintings, some chatting, slowly revolving around the open rooms under the watchful eyes of security guards in velvet jackets. I lost track of the letch and his woman. I was busy listening to Benton explain why he was disappointed.

"It's just, you can't paint a baby. No one can. It'll come out creepy every time. Look, do you want to go to the exhibit now? There's only so many naked babies I can take. It's all the same thing, isn't it? Saints and Jesuses and naked babies. I thought there'd be more modern art. Do you mind?"

I told Benton I didn't mind, and the rest of the rooms went quickly. He was right, of course. Papal propaganda, from one hall to the next. But every moment or so the corner of my eye would catch a new color, a new arrangement, and while Benton pressed on, I would linger, inspecting the painting, imagining the hand the brushstrokes had been made under, wondering how it might have looked in Flemish candlelight. Looking towards the effort.

When I caught up to Benton, he was outside on the balcony, leaning against the railing, looking at his cell phone. Beyond him, Los Angeles in haze, the edges of what we could see blurred, a city out of focus. The ocean was a grey wall, the sky an oyster shell. In the surrounding hills, houses, perched on waiting mudslides, kept their own views. Everyone with a little piece of Los Angeles to see.

"Look," Benton said, pointing down, pretending he hadn't been texting. "Deer."

There were three mule deer on the slopes far below, a buck and two does, nibbling on chamise and ragweed. While Benton and I watched, two women in hijabs put their backs on the balcony next to us. They looked like sisters, practically identical plump faces framed in peach and maroon silks. One woman lifted a selfie stick. They both giggled. The selfie stick shook. I wondered aloud where the deer could go, when all the land around us was accounted for and priced.

"Who knows?" Benton said. "I tried to get a picture, but they're too far away."

I agreed. Everything was too far away, so we left the deer to their shrubs and the sisters to their selfies and retreated inside, to the next pavilion, the one hosting the Koudelka exhibit, Benton's chosen reason for coming.

There was a sign at the exhibit's beginning. I read it; Benton walked on. It told a little about Josef Koudelka, about the things he had seen, the places he had been. Moravia, Romania, lands with fairy tale names, Prague in blood springs, London, Paris, New York, the border of Palestine and Israel. All on the other end of his camera.

I couldn't find Benton. After a while I stopped trying.

Koudelka took pictures. I mean it in the most literal sense. He took them from people, pictures of their lives, moments they were unaware of, their most vulnerable angles, rendered in black and white grains. He took pictures of Roma boys in muscleman poses. He took pictures of grandmothers at the wakes of their granddaughters. He took pictures of vagabonds and actors, clowns and protesters, working men, evening women, musicians at wedding feasts, lovers on cobblestone streets, newlyweds, grieving widows, the infirm, the insane, the clairvoyant and the blind, the emaciated and the drunk, horses with their riders, goats with their herders, men at their cards, women at their knitting, dead birds and broken statues, tanks, Soviet soldiers and Soviet guns, crowds watching armies pass. Koudelka took pictures and gave the negatives back. And I looked at them for a time and caught myself wondering who the people in the pictures were, even when the answer had already been framed.

I took my time with Koudelka. When I was done, I looked for Benton. I found him outside, hiding behind a sandstone column. He was talking on his phone, the palm of his free hand pressed into his free ear, his body bent into his navel, his lips in furious motion. I had to guess Alyssa.

I watched him for as long as it took him to tell her he'd see her soon. I did my best to memorize his features, the sculpted jowls, the beard over the cleft chin, the blunted nose, the adamant eyebrows, the sheen of his modern pompadour. Green witch-hazel eyes under mottled Ray Bans. That day, he wore a faded pink polo with the collar buttons undone so his chest hair had room to breathe. I memorized the circumference of his barrel chest, the taper of his waist, the line of his legs in skinny jeans. I decided he was probably a size eight in driving loafers. I stopped there. I wouldn't be able to remember what I wanted anyway.

He hung up. I approached him as though I'd just found him.

"Alyssa wants dinner. Do you mind if I take you back now? I think this is it. You know what I mean? I think this is either where it ends or, well. You know what I mean?"

I didn't. We walked back to the tram. The Tianjin Number One High Schoolers were in the entry hall, clustered around the gift shop, buying postcards of the things they'd taken pictures of, laughing at one another, with one another, their adolescent bodies clustered together on benches and against walls. The Buddhist monks were not to be seen. Benton asked me what I thought of Koudelka. I forget how I answered.

**gold man review**

# Basil-Mint Ice Cream

### r. m. janoe

You're not supposed to spy on Dad when he's in his study. Peek one eye around the edge of the open doorway. He's behind his desk, talking on his cell phone. Mom's beside the desk, staring at him. The phone falls, thuds onto the blotter. His eyebrows raise so high his forehead wrinkles look like Grandpa's accordion in its case.

"What did they say?" Mom asks.

Dad tells her he's charged... something. Think, *Imbezzlemint?* Wonder what *in-basil-mint* is. Think, *basil and mint?* Mom's eyebrows lower and her upper lip raises on one side like she thinks the idea is disgusting. You don't think it's a good combination either, but you can't remember what basil tastes like.

Ask if basil-mint is a new flavor of ice cream.

*Oops.* You forgot you're not supposed to be spying. They stare at you. Your stomach gets heavy, like every time you get caught.

Mom yells, "Go to your room."

Shuffle away. Listen to them argue.

You're in your room playing crash-up derby with your toy cars when Dad comes in with his serious face on and closes the door. Your tummy drops again. Now, he's going to yell at you. You sit on the floor and steal glances at him from the corner of your eye—he's a big, grumpy giant. He's still in his work clothes. Wonder why he didn't go to work today like normal.

"Hey, Son."

Say hi.

He sits on the bed and rests his elbows on his knees, hands hanging in the air. His lips smile, but his eyes are sad.

"How about we go get some ice cream?"

Usually, work's all he thinks about when he's home. He never ever takes you to get ice cream.

Say yes, then ask if you're in trouble.

"Why would you be in trouble?"

Say because your spying made him and mom argue.

He grunts. "You didn't make us argue. Mom's just mad at me."

Ask if it's because he charged basil-mint ice cream on the credit card.

He stares at you with his mouth all puckered up like you've disappointed him. Wonder if it's because you found out about the ice cream. Wonder if it's because you found out he wasted money on weird ice cream when he makes you save all your Christmas and birthday money in his bank instead of 'wasting it' on toys and candy.

He stares so long you wonder if he got frozen.

"Don't worry about that, Tad. It's just a work thing. Get your coat."

You two go for ice cream after school almost every day for the next few weeks. Dad buys you a bunch of toys and takes you to the park. He doesn't go to work; he says he's taking a vacation. Mom works more. She used to be there when you'd get home from school, but now you only see her when she wakes you up by kissing your forehead and pulling the covers up to your chin.

Ask her where she's been. Say you missed her.

"At work, Dear. I missed you, too. Go back to sleep, now."

Their arguing voices are far away. You sneak downstairs. Watch Mom, red-faced, pointing at Dad. "It's your fault!"

Watch Dad, arms crossed. "You always want mo—"

Listen to the silence ringing. Watch Mom hold her hand like she hurt it on Dad's face. Stare at them staring at each other.

Hurry, run. Run quiet. Back to bed. Think, *it's getting worse.* Lay there as tears leak from your closed eyes and tickle your ears.

Hope old Dad never comes back. Snow is falling. You and Dad get hot chocolates with big marshmallows in them and go to the ice-skating rink. You've done this a lot lately. You didn't know Dad could skate, but he's good at it. Christmas is in a few days. He takes you to see Santa, who's sitting on a big, gold throne. A really tall elf-lady lifts you onto Santa's knee.

"Ho, ho, ho. What do you want for Christmas, Tad?" Dad told the elf-lady your name, but you didn't hear her tell Santa. Think, *maybe Santa really is watching me.*

Say you want Dad to never go back to work, so he can stay the way he is now.

Watch Dad's face get super red, and his eyes get watery.

"Well, you keep being a good boy and I'll see what I can do."

Think, *Santa did it!* Dad hasn't gone back to work. It's getting warmer outside. Yesterday, he bought ice cream cones and took you to the park. The last few weeks you've done that, or walked around the neighborhood together, after you got home from school. He and Mom ignore each other. They rarely talk anymore. Think, *at least they've stopped arguing.*

Today, he takes you to the carnival. You guys ride the rides, including the Ferris wheel, twice, and play some games. You win a swirling yellow-and-white-colored rubber bouncy ball by hitting metal duck targets with a pop gun, and then Dad spends a long time throwing darts at balloons. Dad wins you a big blue monkey you name Jimmy—because *George* isn't blue—then Dad lets you eat hotdogs and cotton candy for dinner.

At home, he tucks you and Jimmy into bed and sits on the edge.

"Son, I have to go away for a while. Take care of your Mom for me until I get back, okay?" His voice and chin quiver.

Ask him why. Say you don't want him to go. Your eyes get blurry, and your throat tightens.

"I know, but I have to."

Ask him how long and where he's going.

"Up state. I don't know, it'll be a while."

Sit up and hug him. Cry, and feel him cry soundlessly in your arms. See tears sparkle on his cheeks in the dim glow of your nightlight as he looks back at you and closes your bedroom door.

# Deathbed Catholic, Directed Panspermia, Big Bang

timothy reilly

> *We dance round in a ring and suppose,*
> *But the secret sits in the middle and knows.*
> Robert Frost

*For Jo-Anne*

## Deathbed Catholic

Terrance Godfrey wanted definitive answers. He dabbled with atheism for a few years but found out the hard way he wasn't a true nonbeliever. The moment of reckoning came when he suffered a severe gallbladder attack and started praying to God to save him from the unbearable pain and possibility of death. *There are no atheists in foxholes,* he reasoned. But after being relieved of his pain (and gallbladder) by laparoscopic surgery, he had to deal with the guilt of backsliding from nonbelief. *Surely, I'd be forgiven for copping out under torture.* He made a point of *not* thanking God. It was something like a penance. But his heart wasn't in it.

Prior to his surgery, Terrance had to fill out several forms—most of which were designed to excuse the hospital and its staff of any legal responsibility, should the patient (for some unforeseen circumstance) not survive this safe and simple procedure. He'd suffered too much pain to quibble—he just wanted to get this thing over with—so he signed and initialed most of the forms without much scrutiny. One form, however, caught him off-guard: a form asking for religious preference. Scanning his choices, he had an involuntary reflex and checked "Catholic." He was relieved when the woman at the desk showed no interest in his choice, but the act of checking that particular box inwardly branded him a *Deathbed Catholic*.

Three days later, while enjoying a speedy outpatient recovery, he decided to counter the Deathbed Catholic stigma by taking refuge in a neutral country: Agnosticism. *I know that I know nothing,* he declared, adjusting his imaginary Greek tunic.

## Directed Panspermia

Years before, in his early thirties, he discovered a TV program inspiring him to become a "Free Thinker." The program was *Cosmos*, and its host was the astrophysicist, Carl Sagan. Terrance liked the sound of *Free Thinker*. It was vague and noncommittal. He would be *free* to *think* as he pleased. He religiously watched all thirteen episodes of *Cosmos*, noting at the end that Dr. Sagan certainly didn't suffer from triskaidekaphobia—or any other superstitious nonsense.

The newly enlightened Terrance enrolled in Sagan's *Planetary Society* and purchased a small Newtonian telescope and some books on amateur astronomy. Focusing his telescope on Saturn, he felt like a child reading on his own for the first time. This little dot of light had been there all along, unadorned to his naked eye, and now he beheld its mysterious rings. *Unbelievable.*

Later, at a party of fellow backyard astronomers, he joined in a roundtable discussion concerning the merits of deism versus theism. He was a bit tipsy, and knew nothing about either -ism, so when asked whether he was a deist or theist, he blurted "I'm an atheist." Although it was a baptism by alcohol, he decided to stick to his hasty choice rather than losing face.

Over the years, he would consume dozens of scientific articles and books marketed for the layperson. He tended to trust this popular literature without question. But shortly after his gallbladder adventure, he had the unsettling realization that most of the scientists he'd read and admired (including Carl Sagan and Stephen Hawking) appeared to be bent on proving that a divine being could not possibly have been the source of kickstarting the universe. Scientists trying to prove the improvable seemed, to Terrance, a completely unscientific endeavor. Add to that the contradictory exercise of endlessly scanning deep space: searching for longshot evidence of *Superior Beings* broadcasting salutations from other worlds. Even Francis Crick, the Nobel Prize recipient and co-discoverer of the molecular structure of DNA, got into the act. Crick authored a book called *Life Itself*, in which he suggests that the molecular "seeds" of what would eventually evolve into human beings, could have purposely been sent to our planet via an ET spaceship. He "labeled" the shipping process "directed panspermia"—implying that the human race was intentionally "planted" on

Earth by loving extraterrestrials. The whole thing reeked of *Star Trek* and the proverbial chicken or egg conundrum.

## Big Bang

To clear his palate of directed panspermia, Terrance decided to return to basics. He pulled from his bookshelf a Beginner's Astronomy book and opened to a chapter titled "In the Beginning was the Big Bang." He was of course revisiting familiar territory, but this time a few previously glossed over details stood out. He remembered having read about Edwin Hubble's major contributions, such as the observation that distant objects, formerly grouped as nebulae, were actually other galaxies in an *expanding universe*, and that the universe itself had *a beginning*. Terrance didn't remember, however, that the Big Bang theory was first posited, in 1927, by the Belgian astrophysicist (and Catholic priest!) Georges Lemaître—who declared that time and space began with a single "primeval atom" containing the total mass of the universe. In fact, the concept of an expanding universe came to be known as the Hubble-Lemaître Law.

Reading on, Terrance came to a section describing the mysterious theory of Dark Matter. No one knows for certain what this invisible stuff is, but it seems to be taking up ninety percent of the universe. Pondering Dark Matter reminded him of when he was nine years old: how he favored a toy that made use of a wand-magnet to manipulate iron filings onto the cartoon headshot of a hairless, androgynous being. He took pleasure in transforming the headshot into likenesses of Abe Lincoln, Groucho Marx, Colonel Schweppes, and Adolf Hitler. He also discovered other uses for the wand-magnet: such as pulling a long train of paper clips, or coaxing brads to scoot across a thin sheet of cardboard. Playing with two magnets, he stumbled upon the phenomenon of *like poles*. No matter how many times he tried to push them together, the magnets refused to meet. He could feel, through his fingers, a powerful invisible force. The discovery of fire could not have been more astounding.

For some reason, this pleasant childhood memory triggered in Terrance an impulse to drive thirty-five miles to the small town in which he'd spent the first twenty years of his life. Driving down the main boulevard of his old haunt, he recognized many of the old buildings but was shocked to see that most of them were now Bar & Grills and tattoo parlors, and that the sturdy Buster Brown Shoe Store had been capsized by a peddler of bail bonds. It was like the scene from *It's a Wonderful Life*, in which George Bailey runs panicking through the streets of Bedford Falls-turned-Pottersville.

Terrance continued driving down to the site of his old elementary school. He was pleased to find it relatively unchanged. For the first time in over sixty years, he walked onto the school's playground and was drawn like a magnet to the traditional centerpiece: a massive California live oak. This was the very tree he and other students would daily gather round during recess. There was always an unspoken code of behavior observed under its sheltering limbs and branches.

Standing there now, he was suddenly taken by an inexplicable sense of yearning, something like the sad and beautiful feeling he experienced whenever he heard Judy Garland sing "Somewhere Over the Rainbow." It had nothing to do with time or space or physics.

"Sir?" a security guard approached him. "I'm sorry, sir. You aren't allowed to be on the school grounds without permission."

That was that. It was obvious he had no legitimate reason to be on this property—at least no reason he could adequately explain. There was no one left at the school who could vouch for him. All his former teachers were dead and gone.

*Gone where?*

He began walking toward the exit gate. He sensed his stint with agnosticism coming to an end.

fiction

# Forever Racing
## ashwin vaidyanathan

Ma had been asking for the old family photo album for weeks. At first, she had tolerated my excuses, even validated them with her tender nods. But it turns out that even the most patient among us have their breaking points. I assured her I would find the album once the football game ended, but the woman who spent hours on end rocking to the cadence of the front porch winds suddenly couldn't wait just five more minutes. A loud bang followed by her faint gasp forces me to set down my beer and run over to the hallway.

The ceiling string to release the attic ladder stairs had been pulled. But without a gentle lowering, the ladder had crashed down, leaving a little divot and scratch in the dull hardwood floor. More concerning, however, was that Ma already had one leg on the first step and was struggling to bring her bum left leg up to the second. A warm pride fills my chest as I marvel at her fighting spirit, but I make sure not to show it.

"Ma, are you crazy? Get down from there!"

"Only when I'm in danger do you decide to be useful, huh?"

I try to maintain an admonishing glare but break into a slight smile. Ma, ever perceptive, notices and laughs as she steps down.

"Well, are you going up? Or do I need to hang upside down from the fifth rung to keep you away from the silly football game?"

"I'm going, I'm going. Don't push your luck."

I gingerly climb up, secretly hoping that the rickety steps can support my newly added weight. Once upstairs, I reach through the cobwebs for the light switch, which causes the hanging bulb in the middle of the room to flicker a couple of times before fizzling out. I add it to the mental list of needed house repairs. But for now, enough sunlight is filtering in through the west-facing window.

I cautiously start opening up boxes, afraid that a spider or rodent might jump out. That fear quickly morphs to boredom, though, as I sift through box after box of knick-knacks, wall decor, and old clothes so ratty and torn they wouldn't even qualify for the Good-will discount bin.

My heart drops as I open a giant box filled with Christmas lights and decorations. Christmas had always been Mark's favorite holiday, and he would spend days setting up elaborate light displays in the front yard. But since his passing, exactly two years to the day, Ma and I hadn't bothered with decorating for the Christmas holidays.

I sit down on an adjacent crate and stare at all my reflections dejectedly glaring back in the ornaments' various colorful hues. Had I let Mark down by not continuing his Christmas traditions? The neighborhood kids had loved Mark's lights displays. I surely could have put in a little effort to preserve and continue his legacy.

"Is that what you want?" I plead, desperately wanting to see Mark instead of myself in the colorful baubles. Not too much of a stretch given we are identical twins. Were identical twins? Two years, and I still don't know how to describe the situation.

I add Christmas decorating to the growing list of to-dos but refocus now on the most urgent task of finding the photo album. The cool October sun has almost set below the horizon, and with each unsuccessful opening, my regret for not labeling the boxes grows.

With just a few unopened boxes remaining, I finally find the photo album tucked away below some hats. The faux leather cover is instantly recognizable given how often I used to leaf through the album when I was younger. But now, I'm reluctant to open it. I'm still not ready to see Mark's toothy smile again. Anyway, better to have Ma open it first.

Mission accomplished, I go around the room closing all the boxes when I notice my old Wii gaming device. I stack the white console, remote controllers, and cables on the photo album and make my way down the ladder, carefully matching both feet on each step down.

Ma at first stares indignantly at the Wii but lightens up into a smile when she notices the photo album below it. She turns the stove down to a simmer, leaving the big pot of chili to tend to itself as she shifts her attention to the book. I place the album in her outstretched arms, then turn back to the living room.

"You already looked through the photos?" Ma asks surprised.

Reminiscing through old photos of Mark may help Ma process and move on, but I fear that it might have the opposite effect on me. I don't know how to put this fear into words, though, so I instead just nod and continue out of the kitchen.

In the living room, I kneel down in front of the television and plug in the Wii. The setup goes smoothly, with only one Google assist required to check how to hook up the motion sensor. I change out the batteries in the Wii remote, then power on the console. The iconic homepage melody starts playing, which triggers endless memories of virtual adventures with Mark. The times we collected Grand Stars in Super Mario Galaxy, scored goals in FIFA, and shot down enemy tanks in Wii Play come rushing back. But those games all pale in comparison to the countless hours we spent on Mario Kart. The thrill of beating Mark, combined with some lighthearted trash talking, could brighten up even the worst of days.

It's no surprise that the disc in the Wii is Mario Kart since it was the last game we played. My whole body shakes in anticipation, which makes selecting the game with the motion-controlled remote more challenging. Once I do, I click into the single player time trials mode and select Mark's favorite course, Koopa Cave. Cruising through the river currents reminded Mark of kayaking, one of his favorite hobbies growing up.

The race countdown begins, but I mess up the timing and miss out on the starting boost. A ghostly character gets the boost instead and shoots out ahead. Realizing what happened, I eagerly call Ma, who limps over as quickly as she can.

"What's wrong?"

I try to answer, but all I can do is point at the screen and repeatedly stutter, "It's Mark, it's Mark!"

Ma stares at the screen, still confused, so I compose myself and try again.

"Mario Kart saves the single best time trial for every course. That ghostly figure is really Mark's best run of this course. I'm racing against him again!"

Ma nods, "But how do you know that's Mark's ghost and not your best time ghost?"

"If I beat the ghost, then it will be replaced with my best run. But right now, it is clearly Mark's ghost because of how it's driving,"

I reply, refocusing on the race. "Mark always drifted aggressively to get the boosts, even when the turns aren't that sharp like in this part of the course."

The reply probably doesn't mean much to Ma, but I am clearly happy, and nothing can ruin that. She sits down next to me, equally joyful as she flips through the old photos. By the time the first race ends, the ghost is nowhere in sight as I am a whopping twenty seconds behind. I know I am capable of beating Mark's ghost, but I will need to practice. A lot.

Over the next few weeks, I play religiously, one race each night. After each race, I look back fondly on some memory of Mark. No longer with spite and hatred at the world for taking him away too soon, but now with joy and gratitude for the moments that we did get to spend together.

Sixty-four days after that fateful attic search, I drive a flawless race. I hit every boost, nail every jump, and perfect every turn. For the first time, I see the finish line with no ghost ahead of me. Just a straightaway with no more obstacles or chances to lose. But instead of keeping my finger on the accelerator button, I loosen up. My car starts slowing down, and with just a few feet to the finish line, Mark's ghost zooms ahead, preserving its place in the time trial history.

"Keep on racing," I whisper to my brother. "The world awaits."

At peace, I unplug the Wii and place it in the box of items to be returned to the attic. I hear some kids laughing outside and go out to the snow-dusted front porch. Ma is bundled up in jackets and blankets, rocking away in her trusty chair. Together, we look out at the magnificent display lighting up our front yard and wish the awestruck kids a Merry Christmas.

# Legend of the Lengendary Poetry
### (find titles to play)


Our Valley

The Revenge of Things

Escondido

The Red Wheelbarrow

Sonnedizio Sweetness

Gummy Bears

Instructions in the Event

This Is A Pond Because I Want It To Be

The Whispered Ones

# GOLD POETRY SCRAMBLE

```
I F Q E J U K N N U H C G U I N G S
T U J D E A E S C O N D I D O J U M
H S U I N S T R U C T I O N S O M S
I H I R G U U R D W H N G M R S M O
S B I L L R V O L T E V E N T G Y N
I W E H U A L E T P I K T K T U B N
S W I N L O W S H C K S H M U O E E
A D O L P E N T E L T G E N I P A D
P F E F E L T U R M Y D W H O O R I
O Y R E V E N G E O F E H I N G S Z
N I H G Y N I G D R N T I H G Y N I
D S U U T G O D W N H H S U U T G O
B P M W R E S U H G E N P M W R E S
E E I I H G Y N E E G J E I E F Y W
C R O S U U T E E G U U R O C H T E
A E L P M W R W L U W I E L T D T E
U D P E I E F E B W E L D P Y N Y T
S I H G Y N I O A E N O O G U G J N
E S U U T G O N R N G S N E I E M E
I P M W R E S L R G E D E V I Y F S
W E I E F Y W N O E U R S E F T G S
A R O C I H G Y W I W F D N H W D U
N E L T S U I N S T R U C T I O N S
T D P Y P M N R E H N Y C F K T G I
I F U J E I E F Y E N E V E E H T N
T T O B E O C H T E E B F G R H I H
```

# Pepper Spaghetti Sauce

## Provided by Editor, Eric Halpenny
## (his own recipe)

### Ingredients

2-3 tbsp olive oil
1 onion, diced
1 red bell pepper, diced
1 tbsp tomato paste
1/4 tsp black pepper
2 tsp oregano
1/8 tsp red pepper flakes (more to taste)
1/4 tsp kosher salt
28 oz can of tomato puree + 1 can of cold water

### Directions

1. Heat olive oil over medium heat until it shimmers. Add diced onion and pinch of salt. Saute until tender and translucent (2-4 minutes).
2. Add tomato paste and cook for 1 minute
3. Add bell pepper and spices. Saute stirring for 2-3 minutes or until peppers start to soften.
4. Add tomato puree; use water to rinse the can into the sauce; add 1/8 tsp of baking soda to reduce chance of heartburn/acid reflux.
5. Bring sauce to a simmer, reduce heat to maintain slow simmer. Let sauce simmer for 30 min (at least) or 1-2 hours.
6. Serve with cooked pasta.

# Our Valley

eileen pettycrew

Let me go back
to that ruinous land.
Let the oleander
bathe me in its arms.
Let me see my parents
waking early, salt already
in their wounds.
Let me walk the dirt roads
while heat waves work
the field like migrants.
I want a tractor stamped
with my father's handprints,
broad-leafed weeds wilting
under my mother's hoe.
I want a good price
on potatoes, a well
that never runs dry.
I want cotton
too stubborn to die,
a crop duster in the distance
laying down its bright
carpet of fume.
Let me tumble in their lives
like a dust storm.
I want the last drop
of my father's sweat,
the last stitch
of my mother's needle.
I want to feel
the infinity of this place
like a prayer I never said,
like oil derricks in the night
hoisting their cold cargo of stars.

poem

# The Revenge of Things

joel savishinsky

> "Nothing any longer adheres to life; it is
> this painful cleavage which is responsible
> for the revenge of things."
> -Antonin Artaud, *The Theater and Its Double* (1938)

They are winning. Perhaps they have
already won. When Thoreau observed
that men have become the tools of
their tools, he wrote of a time whose
implements would now strike us as toys.
The wounds they could inflict would
only cut the body; our century's devices
corrode the senses, unwire the soul.
There is no longer a day of rest:
what once were seven sanctities are
now neither numbered or named,
just marked by fears inflected
with different degrees of urgency.

In a place where everything is post
something else, *what comes to hand*
takes the heart out of the body and
the body out of the world, launches
the heart itself till its recession is
an errant satellite lost in space.
*What comes to mind* are bits of thought
that once were words, sound-bytes
strung on thread sewing lips together,
the new craft of the valley's oral surgeons.

*What comes to pass* is the unclaimed surplus
of our imaginations, desperate investments in
gadgets born in fever dreams, blunt instruments
of self-injury. *What comes to call* in this endless
year of Pavlov's Dog, whose envy trumps hunger,
is a continuous call-and-response, a chorus that
demands we forgo the past and its poetries.

*What comes ashore* are the remnants of all our
one-night stands, plastic dreams that leave us
rapt in awe, bubbles that burst the song of birds
and the bellies of whales. *What comes to rest*
defies sleep, edits regret with the machinery
of memory, gloats in shadows where
its neon pulse needles tattoos on the retina.

*What comes to stay* cannot rest, sports
a necklace whose twitching lights signal
a search for the ever, never now, its rhymes
rhythmically feeding that failure of nerve
we have all known since adolescence.
*What comes to be* could have been a leaf
but never made it past the secret code,
features a drumroll of promises that pulled up
its walking-stick roots, that found no traction
or stomach for the struggle, that each morning
since the Fall has abandoned all its mystery.

It turns out the discards –
   the hip pocket pacifiers,
      these never-let-me-go worry beads,
         those rosaries for the new age of anxiety –
have been collecting us all along.
Trying to add up the sum of our parts, however,
their calculus has failed: they cannot differentiate
product from hope, function from sign. Their steps
show how the shape of things to come has come
and gone. It came to nothing, an empty case
displayed in the long hallway of hubris.

# Escondido

judd hess

Of course I love you, back alley and chaparral.
I love you the way Mama Cruz loved me,
the way a nest does an orphaned egg.

I invite you, shy one, with horchata to a porch.
On your birthday, I and the manzanita trees
will push your sunburnt face into a cake.

We can sit the languid afternoon like rabbits.
I will sweep tarantulas from our under-rafters
with a broom. I will listen to your dusty smiles.

Learn that you matter: that simplest and most
elusive homestead. Let your barred windows
be as magnificent as your wildfire seasons.

One day you too will be an old woman: iron
and wholeness. You too will bristle with
junipers, and, with tortillas hechas a mano,

wrap a broken thing in welcome. Hide him
in your skirts. Pay forward how you were
succored a long summer under my feathers.

# The Red Wheelbarrow

## toni la ree bennett

There are so many things
that could fill this red wheelbarrow.

If you put something in
and I put something in
we could erase the space
blaming us for its emptiness.

Are you willing to part with
something you can't bear to lose
so that it can join with mine
and we can wheel it away
far from here, hide it behind the barn
or dump it in a ditch
where weather will later obscure
any marker of its burial
and we will never see it again.

Are you and I that brave?

# Sonnedizio Sweetness

### r. thursday

After Kim Addonizio

*We're good at kissing, we like how that part goes,*
it goes like this: the hero hunter strides towards
the treasure, call it gold, all soft, heating quickly -
drips glowing stars like freckles anointed, a wide
brush, you said, goading lips across cheekbones,
nose; I should have admitted I sought to bless
more of your spotted topography, grow more
map hits with my breath, inspire more goose
bumps, but still, the going is good, too (like Super
man, I resist saying, resist comparison), the gone
is not forever, and besides, the goal was never so
gauche as bonsai-binding, and besides I still
feel the tender go before my teeth, bruise and cause,
wearing your kiss like a breath devouring gown.

# Gummy Bears

**kory vance**

Knock-knock — Hello
We're here for gummy bears
And salvation

Our planet is at war
And we're scared
We need your peace
And satiation

On the doorstep of a church, a family of little, round aliens smiled at Pastor Bob. Their skin was plump and it squished in at the touch like a bunch of jelly was ready to burst out. They all wore wire-framed glasses with lenses that were two-inches thick. Even the two kids and the little tiny baby, who looked like a blueberry, wore glasses. As the wind blew, the liquid inside them made their skin ripple. The aliens smiled through it.

Pastor Bob was at the door, introducing the aliens to our planet and his nation. It was humanity's first encounter, the beginning of an alien invasion. The alien invasion was for gummy bears and salvation.

Knock-knock — Hello
You spoke with care
In your oration

We were sitting here
On the stairs
You said church is a refuge
And we exhaled with elation

Pastor Bob was almost bald. He had been polishing the church's collection plates when he heard the knock. That morning, while his freckled wife was still asleep, Pastor Bob sat on the toilet stretching the skin on the back of one hand so his wrinkles disappeared for a moment. At breakfast, he had dry cereal and coffee while quietly jotting in his prayer journal:

*God, please impart on the congregation the spirit of generosity so we may build a new sanctuary.
*God, please help me focus more on the Kingdom than on the money.
*God, please remove from my heart these sinful desires for the Lamberts' young daughter back from college.
*God, please bless me and our church family with the opportunity to share your love and grace.

Knock-knock — Hello
Our eyes are blue with despair
We need your communication

You've said nothing
We're cold in your air
We need your candy
For hydration

The little aliens' home planet almost exclusively grew corn. It was basically corn. The red kernels grew individually on vines instead of cobs. Most of the economy was based on harvesting the kernels and extracting syrup. The little jelly aliens sustained themselves by filling up their plump bodies.

In a neighboring galaxy, the inhabitants had long whiskers and eight limbs, each with a spiny pincer on the end. Their bodies were covered in long yellow feathers. The Pincer-People considered the corn syrup a delicacy, so they put on their atmosphere masks and traveled to the planet's vineyards. In a matter of days, they popped half the population like grapes in their pincers.

Knock-knock — Hello
We're here for gummy bears
And salvation

Our planet is at war
And we're scared
We need your peace
And satiation

# Instructions in the Event...

## priscilla long

When I'm gone,
look for me in *poems*
*without words*, in corners
missing their rooms.
Look for me in the sun-struck afternoon
this rainstorm can't remember.
Look for me in some Metsker Maps
shop crammed with the faded,
folded maps of my imagination,
roads rubbed out, signposts
too tiny to read. Look for me
in the crease between Pennsylvania
and postmodern discourse. Try
that underground dive where
Hazel Dickens belts out *You'll get*
*no more of me*, which gets mixed
up with Julio Cortázar speaking
my mind in Spanish: *Don't*
*let me fade away*
*like some stupid song...*

poem

# This Is A Pond Because I Want It To Be

raul herrera jr.

As you read this / my mind may be in Mercury again / body chewed inside the mouth / of a new hunger / but regardless of flesh / welcome to this place / of water-lillied words / and the light earnest dancing of fish / This pond is mine-made / the fish hooks / I wrote myself / a family of frogs / giddy behind the pickerel / the sun / scribbled across their tiny faces / and a June bug / sitting atop a stiff log / slowly drifting along / just because I want it to / I welcome you / to greet this quiet living / of eyes that never dry / fins that learn to fly / we are not only meant for swimming / the breeze / I leave / half written / a small sea / a stream of vision / I've erased myself outside this place / just because I wanted to.

# The Whispered Ones

claire scott

We are the whispered ones
the *almosts,* the *not quites,*
the *if onlys,* the *what ifs,*
written in declensions of sorrow,
dwelling in an astatic world
where shadows drift. Can you
hear us when you walk
into a room and for just a moment
forget why you are there, in the silence
of the first star where time's seams
separate and possibilities
linger, the soft pause between
an inhale and exhale, the loft
of your lover's hair, the soles of the wind.
Listen.
The world is a short place.
We are still here in the past
of your future, waiting.
Listen.
Dare to look back.
There are no pillars of salt.

## Legend of the Lengendary Nonfiction
### (You're welcome to use any color combination you want)


### Field Notes: Bi-Mart, 9:20 On a Workday Morning
### (1)
### White

### Body: A Defintion
### (2)
### Blue

### What Happened When I Tried to Clone My Cat
### (3)
### Brown

### Elephant Baths
### (4)
### Gray

### Mother Land
### (5)
### Green

### The First
### (6)
### Brown

# Peach-Strawberry Upside-Down Cake

## Provided by Editor, Eric Halpenny
## (his own recipe)

### Cake
1/2 cup butter
3/4 cup brown sugar
3/4 cup white sugar
2 eggs
1 tsp vanilla
2 cups flour
1/2 tsp baking powder
1 tsp baking soda
1 cup sour cream or Greek yogurt
2 cups diced peaches tossed in 1-2 Tbsp of flour
Pinch of salt

### Topping
1/4 cup melted butter
1 cup packed brown sugar
2 cups sliced strawberries
2 cups diced peaches (with or without skin)

### Directions

1. Preheat oven to 350ºF and grease a 9x13" baking dish all the way to the rim
2. Pour the melted butter into the 9x13" dish and completely coat the bottom.
3. Sprinkle brown sugar evenly. Press strawberries and peaches gently into the sugar until distributed evenly.
4. In a bowl, cream the butter and sugars for the cake. Mix in eggs and vanilla and whip until fluffy
5. Add all dry ingredients and mix slowly. Once flour disappears, add in sour cream (or yogurt).
6. Stir in flour-coated peaches gently.
7. Drop dollops of batter onto the fruit in the dish and carefully spread and fill in holes. The batter is sticky so take care not to pull fruit off of the bottom. Make sure batter touches all sides of the dish.
8. Bake for 40-50 minutes at least. It should be golden brown and a toothpick should come out clean.
9. Allow to cool on a rack for 10 minutes. Use a butter knife to separate the edge all the way around from the dish.

To serve: Hold the cake pan in one hand with your other hand fully supporting the bottom of the dish. Place an inverted serving platter over the top that is larger than the baking dish. Keep your other hand firmly planted on the serving platter. In one smooth motion, invert the cake so the serving dish is on the bottom. The cake will fall directly onto the serving dish. Replace any fruit that may have been left behind. Serve plain or with ice cream.

# Elephant Baths

## m. kolbet

For anyone over thirty-five—who's not a disgruntled wildlife biologist or fervid animal activist—visiting Oregon's zoo is usually a chore. An educational trip. A day praying about weather and nap times. A chance to dodge crowds and wonder if things were always so busy.

One's childhood memory doesn't divulge such details. One's adult memory, prematurely weary, suggests it could never be otherwise.

What's needed is a better coat. The current one has lost is signature puffiness. "Clean linen for the backs of thieves," says a line of poetry from Richard Wilbur. While the coat still slouches past the hips, it feels too much like smooth, untrustworthy skin. This isn't the life anyone's parents imagined, and most people, with their seized looks, don't seem sure how to live it.

Charts and measurements work against the moment. It's no good thinking how near one's next birthday is, how many years have passed since visiting the zoo, or how many strokes it would take to cross the elephant bath. In the pool, where rising steam speaks of heat, the beasts luxuriate. All descriptions begin to seem doubtful, whether the roundness of a sloped shoulder or the clarity of a patch of sky. The recognition that a pachyderm's eye is only slightly larger than a human's. Even setting a chronicle is insignificant. The mind cannot trust everything it carries. There are no terms to quantify enchantment, and such appetites grow the more they are fed.

This spectacle of tumbling brutes is a bigger yet more gentle version of professional wrestling. Even wrestle may be a word of too much clamor. The elephants don't need costumes or gimmicks. Swinging chairs. Instead, they use their trunks to shoot water over their shoulders during a rear-guard attack. The playful battles are cyclical, but because they're animals, their wildness barely contained by an enclosure, it doesn't seem as predictable or sterile as anything on television. Like mountains that transform between seasons and with proximity—landmarks in the distance and immobile leviathans on approach—there's no getting accustomed to them, to the way they go on "keeping their difficult balance" Wilbur notes in the same poem, where he writes of nuns in dark habits.

Every time one of the five-ton beasts rolls on top of its companion, briefly submerging its faux foe, visitors exclaim. Another tumultuous escape. They've seen it, but each new iteration is more than replay.

Elephant hides are often more than two centimeters thick, composed of long fibers. It can retain ten times as much water as gawkers with flat skin. And because this is play, it's more like art. Nothing mundane. Nothing mechanical. The three-hundred pounds of food an elephant eats each day may astound, but it's not magical. The corresponding amount of poop even less so.

The eye has unhindered range, yet returns to shifting legs and trunks in the large pool where there are no islands to steady them. One looks for reminders that elephants have an inside, how they know their own forms. Still, to watch them is to discover properties in the self, a spirit as naked as their bulking masses.

Theirs is the kind of joy that could make you forget it was only two weeks into January when you broke your resolutions, joining a woeful chorus the world over. Drinking. Sex. Old habits. Tumbling elephants argue vehemently against the idea of past as prologue. There can be new whorls, new patterns. If they slip, make an error in judgment, no one judges. Coming to see the elephants, one recalls other places, though few, where there is no sense of fear. Where the spirit leapt, not worried it would concuss against a ceiling or another traveler. Where every fall was but a moment, and into yielding water. One's spirit never drowns during baptism.

The distraction will not last. Soon the elephants will trundle back to the open flat of the yard. Or into private quarters. Here the greatest good for the greatest numbers does not matter. Visitors will eventually shuffle off, too.

Before an end, time to listen. Not to the occasional grunts of the elephant or Henry Mancini or circus themes, but to the lack of destination. In a zoo, for visitors there is no place one has to be. Sound disintegrates: a few raindrops come down like so many early plums. Nearby, they turn into a trickle from a gutter. The elephants slap the water with their trunks and almost seem to laugh. There is a pliancy to the surface of the lake, a grace in the creatures, and neither seems to fear the other. A watching child snorts.

The sky clouds, and a few more drops fall; guests slowly raise umbrellas. It is less protest and more an acknowledgement of the sky's power. Children may dance, offer small complaints of hunger or other biological needs; with a word, they wait. In this hiatus from roofs and bright rooms and forced air, they learn first, or again, of what will can achieve.

Rain falls harder. People seek to make themselves smaller, for like the chill, the rain is persistent, condensing on exposed hair, sliding off old coats and bare hands. The elephants do not mind. They don't appear to notice. Instead, they make cataracts of their own from the warm, manmade lake. Wet and noisy, it is like a morning of first birth, where origins are majestic culmination and fading lines and lovely dreams all at once.

Is it still morning? The sun is too shy to make the claim.

The elephants do not try to escape the steeper sides, the lake pushing against an artificial bluff, a last feeble attempt to hold them. Perhaps the lake drops off, more moat than anything, at the edge. Together, they might be able to clamber out, one hoisting the other. Yet elephants see most with their trunk. Those eyes, replicated in humans, catch a world only twenty-five feet away, and watchers like us are simply dark shadows on a dim day, too diminutive to be a threat.

Above, squawking birds in late migration catch the elephants' attention. Avian footprints will last as long in the air as those left in water by weightier brutes.

And just like that, all concludes. The elephants slip away first, as if adept at reading clouds. Rain intensifies. Parents gather children and foment enthusiasm for an animal—less lively, of course—under a roof and behind glass.

But even conclusion is a misnomer. Shared time has changed the most watchful pilgrims, who leave in wayward ripples, their feet and the rain wreathing over the pavement. There is no end to lovely things. No miserable imprisonment of time.

An errant wind blows.

nonfiction

# Mother Land
ekaterina suvorova

Mom often spoke of Russia. Of the golden summers. Of the sweet apples that grew at her babushka's *dacha*. Her eyes glittered as she remembered exploring the thick forest, her fingers covered in gummy sap gifted to her by the birch trees. She wove such beautiful stories of our motherland that even though I didn't remember our country, I missed it too. When I asked her how we could leave such a beautiful place she told me that although Russia loved us, she was sick. Russia gave us all she could, Mom said, but it wasn't enough.

After the fall of the Soviet Union, my dad convinced Mom to travel with him to the Netherlands. She was surprised not to see Dedushkas on the street, selling their World War II medals for a few Kopecks to buy *Pirozhki s Kapostoy* to eat. Her eyes widened at the food on the shelves, plump and clean. The clothes, without holes.

Life doesn't have to be so hard, she realized. But she couldn't leave. Russia needed her children to believe in her.

Mom worked honestly—as a teacher, doing her best to help nurture the Russian soul in each child she taught. The soul that sprouted as soon as your first cries watered the Russian soil, she told me. The soul that's passed from our ancestors who tilled the harsh winter earth, to us, who are meant to enjoy its fruits.

As time went on, our country's illness from political corruption spread, the fruit from her bounty souring. Oligarchs emerged, their interests not in the Russian soul but in the resources they could leech from their motherland. The country's own children were mauling her to stay alive—the same children Mom taught to love Russia needed guns to endure her.

Still, Mom stayed.

Mom gave up teaching after she had me. She was pouring a vodka in the kitchen of the casino she worked at when she heard the pop of bullets against the metal kitchen doors. This is it, she thought. This is how I die. She didn't know what came over her—maybe it was the Russian Soul—but something told her to run to the freezer.

Time slowed, or maybe it was the cold, but what kept her alive was her heart thudding the syllables of my name. Eventually she left the freezer, but the cold had already burrowed inside of her, making a home in her skin.

Mom said goodbye to the maternal soil that held her as she learned to walk, where I took my first steps, for a place we could barely stand.

We went from belonging, to being undocumented immigrants. We were each other's refuge. Pockets of familiarity and safety among people who called her a whore and me a leech as she wove through men, looking for citizenship and security in each one. America so clearly didn't want us, but Mom kept chipping away at herself, giving the country pieces of her flesh in exchange for the hope that one day, even if we didn't fit, we could live in this country without fear.

Mom plucked me from Russia's earth at just the right time, and replanted me quickly, somewhere where the ground was fertile, where she knew opportunities would grow like flowers around me. Mom tried to thread her roots in the United States, but she was already too thoroughly saturated with the loam from her motherland. I was able to grow in America, but she cut herself down until only the part that knew how to survive was left. She began to poison herself, downing whatever she could find: pills, alcohol, anything that numbed the pain. The more years that separated her from her Russia, the more she lost herself fighting for us to stay.

I love my mother. I love how she took me to pick raspberries at the beginning of each summer, our faces sticky and our bellies full as she placed her hand on my chest and told me my soul is Russian, despite where I grew up. I love how her accent chopped English in half, her Russian roots growing over this foreign language trying to take their place.

America gave my mother enough sustenance to endure, but barely. Her veins were interlaced with mine so intricately that they formed a hard knot. I poured into her, giving her what I had to try and save her. I was attempting to replace the pieces of her that America took with the pieces of me that grew here. The parts she dreamed I would grow.

You don't owe her your life just because she brought you here, my friend said, each of her words a seed.

I imagined what my life would look like if I wasn't constantly picking her wilted body from the ground, draining her veins of alcohol.

I couldn't do it. I believed in her too much. I thought she would get better.

Together, we maneuvered through the American dream side by side, with no one else. We were each other's only source of comfort in the chaos that was undocumented immigration, stepfathers, abuse. I had a plethora of families call me their flower. Try and take credit when I bloomed. But my mother was the only person who I could truly be myself around.

You can't keep doing this, I told her, as I planted her flaccid body in her bed. I told myself that if only she didn't have my stepfathers, if only she had a job, if only she had an American degree, if only we had our Green Cards, she would be healthy. She'd be okay.

I can do whatever I want, she answered. I'm your mother.

America had dug a hole and left her to rot.

With delicate fingers I carefully unwound my roots from hers.

She cleared the cobwebs, swept my path, and watched as I walked away.

# Field Notes: Bi-Mart, 9:20 On a Workday Morning

### barb lachenbruch

B i-Mart: Eighty-five stores in the Northwest, bright open spaces, imperceptible music, friendly staff in red or blue smocks—and stuck in the past.

But I have to go there. Our Kmart closed, our Fred Meyer won't have what I'm looking for, and I know the store is easy to navigate once I get past the red gate, the in-my-face greeter, and my attitude.

Because I've tiptoed in a few times—and there's nothing exactly wrong with the place. It has a simple parking lot—no flattened plantings, no curbs. It has wide aisles and an unassuming layout: electronics to the right, housewares straight in front, with hardware behind. Food and pharmacy are on the left, with camping and sports behind all that. And they always have potting soil out front. Nothing will ever change.

But I hear, "Bi-Mart, no. You don't shop there. It's for retirees. Good for plastic bins and sometimes hardware." The voice is Sally from three decades ago. She was my new friend. She'd been orienting me to Corvallis, telling me the shortcuts for getting from Point A to Point B.

I'd just relocated from Berkeley with my husband, our toddler, and our infant. We'd already bought a historic house and launched into its renovations. I had a new position as an assistant professor in a field that was a banana step beyond my expertise. I'd be the first female professor in the department—and, as it turned out, the *only* female professor in the department for the next nineteen years.

I'd found daycare, but not diaper service—but the daycare wouldn't permit cloth diapers anyway. I'd found friendly people and enclaves of liberals, but no one who had a late start on the tenure clock, like I did, because of adventures they took before. But I wasn't looking hard. Getting from Point A toward Point B took all I had.

"Fred Meyer. That's where you'll find everything," Sally had said, and that's where I've been shopping for thirty years.

Consider with me the years as double slips of wax paper into which the memories are pressed. Let us hold each one to the light.

I see young children in primary-color clothing. They're rolling on tricycles beyond our picket fence. I see 4-H potlucks in our living room where doggy-loving people and peculiar packages are spread on our flowered carpet for the doggy gift exchange. In front of me on a trail too steep, I see my husband's backpack. Behind me, I see my son, who's trooping, and my daughter swinging Lambie in her hand. I see business trips afar and airports and vast grocery stores with foreign labels and nothing the kids will eat. I see my husband's company parties—raucous, sometimes luxuriant. Ah, there's our authentic French farmhouse during the first sabbatical—with nothing nearby where my husband says he can work. And there's the tract home in Chile where he could have worked if he had wanted. I see an emptier Corvallis house after the divorce. The flowered carpet and the children are among the remnants that stay.

More little wax-paper windows: a small conference room for committee meetings, filled mostly with men. Computer monitors that are small, then large, then double. A trail through oak savannah with a new friend. He carries a metal thermos of hot chocolate that I can still taste. Bleachers for various graduations, my new husband at my side. That jumble—it's Mom and Dad's boxes and furniture on their move to Corvallis. Their rental house is for Over-55's. The smaller pile, their move to Independent Living; smaller yet, Assisted Living; even smaller, the first of the Adult Foster Homes, where Mom, smiling her brightest, will die. And here's my new ID card, with *Emeritus Faculty* printed as large as my name. My office whiteboard, listing the papers I still want to write. My son handing their chinchilla to his wife so he can instruct me on pet-sitting. My daughter trying to be patient as she explains the keypad for her apartment. Dad, in the garden of his second Adult Foster Home. He's gesturing from his wheelchair about the wonderous sky.

I see so many wax-paper windows I can't keep them separate. My view is opaque.

My daughter's old bedroom is what I see now. You can see it, too. Boxes and files are piled on the bed and half the floor. Loose papers, brochures, diplomas. Stacks of photos curled into one another. And those bundles of letters, the rubber bands withered to dotted lines.

The two milk crates against the window are already crammed with files holding Mom and Dad's memorabilia. You are correct in imagining my sigh.

If I am to sort any more, I need file boxes. Those see-through plastic ones would be handy.

That's where Bi-Mart comes in.

Bi-Mart doesn't open particularly early, but there are a dozen vehicles in the lot when I arrive at 9:20 on a Wednesday morning. Inside, I push through the swinging gate, then look down to deflect the "Hi, welcome" from the red-uniformed greeter. I withdraw a shopping cart, veer right to electronics-slash-office supplies. I place four plastic file boxes in my cart.

By all rights, I should now push the cart to the checkout, pay, and depart.

I can't draw myself to go.

I start in sundries. Everything is familiar: spatulas, Corning ware, cutlery trays. But I get no shopping traction. I don't want to be here: it's a workday even though I'm no longer paid.

I wander past plumbing toward paints. I cut across to Coleman sleeping bags, then turn toward toilet seat extenders. I return to electronics-slash-office supplies where I started. I pick up markers, put them down.

I need nothing further.

Why I can't go, I don't understand.

I follow a woman in a straw hat, but from one aisle over. When she's at sheets and I'm at yarns, I split away. At catches, screws, and hooks, I make small talk with a woman in loose blue pants that can only be called *dungarees*. She's sixtyish and squat. "I've always had good luck with Command," she tells me and holds up a pack that reads "3M Command." These are plastic hooks that will stick to a wall. I put two packs in my cart.

A couple with a stroller streak in front of picnic tables. A woman with a walker inches toward the cash register. She has a chiffon scarf laced through her hair. A gray-haired lady rushes past me, audibly fretting. Her tailored purple dress looks out of place. I think it's pretty, but out of date. She stops, rushes in another direction, and stops again. I'd say she's lost her compass. Here's a gentleman by pretzels with a sports jacket over his t-shirt. And here's a man with a faded vest that has the name of my former employer on it. I knew him. He retired before I'd ever mouthed the word *retire*. I turn away in case he recognizes me.

Some of the shoppers lift items and place them into carts. Others inspect items in their carts and put them back on shelves. Others stop to talk—with anyone: the person they came with, another shopper, or a re-stocker who's looking pleased to pause mid-bustle to now become a docent.

I don't want to take a re-stocker's time. And my cart holds "plastic bins and sometimes hardware," which is more than I came for.

The checkout woman recites a script to the man before me on how to swipe his card. Now she uses the script on me. I decide she has worked here so long that management can't tell her she needs to loosen up.

My cart is aimed at the exit, but my arms steer it left to where a woman, nametagged Amanda, shouts, "Hi" and "Welcome."

"I have some questions," I start, but I don't know what they are. "Is this place just for retired people?" She crooks her neck up and laughs. "No. But yes."

I say I hear they're good for plastics and hardware, and she laughs some more. She's worked here seventeen years. "I bought in," she explains. "Employee-owned."

Has the store changed? "Not much."

What's the target clientele? "We do get a lot of the older people. Especially for Lucky Number Tuesdays."

I've never heard of Lucky Number Tuesdays, and Amanda is surprised. "The grand winner this coming week will get an RCA Security Floodlight Camera. Twenty winners will get a Cool Daddy deep fat fryer, a Cuisinart toaster, a lawn trimmer, or a dashboard camera; and one in ten customers who show their card will get a Little Trees Car Freshener, which comes in a packet of three.—Hi," she tells a couple. "Welcome."

I ask what Bi-Mart does to attract the seniors. "Conservative everything—I don't mean politics." She looks at the many rings on her fingers. "No one's said my rings are a problem. But no green hair. We're not trendy; we carry the basics. Clothes that are easy to put on. Sundries people need, inexpensive. We add a personal touch. I know more than half the people who walk through the door."

Which brings me to the red gate. What's it for? "We're a membership store. Some stores are stricter than others. We're not strict, but you need your card to return something." She shows me the beam of light across the gate that counts the people as they come through. "Fourteen hundred people yesterday," she says. "'Course, it was a Tuesday."

She's tickled when I ask if I might write about what she told me. I tell her I had a bias against the store but that my bias is changing. And can I take and use her picture? "Of course," she says and stretches out her fingers with all the rings.

"Hi, and welcome," she says before I'm sure I've snapped the photo. Then she tells a very short man where to find plungers. "See," she says. "That's what they like about us."

I never thought I'd be retired. Retired—as in working on papers but not being paid, yes. But retired—as in shopping at Bi-Mart, no. I'm in my sixties but never thought I'd be in the same demographic as the woman in the dungarees. But my wax paper collage is the same as hers and yours: memories of getting from Point A to Point B.

I turn from the welcome station. I watch the short man totter toward plungers. Some shoppers talk. Some walk. Some are bewildered. I am all of those. I am all of them.

Now I know why I'm at Bi-Mart. I'm searching for Point C.

# What Happened When I Tried to Clone My Cat

layla schubert

*This wasn't Schrödinger's Cat. He was definitely dead.*

Ferdinand, AKA the Lord of Lard, the Amir of Adiposity, the Corporal of Corpulence, the Prince of Portliness, or simply The Thicktator, was my best buddy for twelve years. Our relationship was based on tormenting squirrels, canned meat, and long naps. Many cats have stalked through my life, but none quite like him. He was a big, fluffy black Tom with satiny fur and scheming green eyes. A lazy, lethargic kitten who had chosen to gather dust on my lap instead of furiously murdering thin air with his brothers and sisters, for Ferd, sucking up to his human family was a contact sport–and he played to win. He grew (and grew and GREW) into the most intelligent cat I've ever met–self-aware enough to conspire with his reflection in the mirror–and he used all of his smarts to indulge his gluttony and to harm smaller animals. When he developed an aggressive mouth cancer and had to be put down after six months of treatment, I was gut-punched.

The next day, listlessly scanning the headlines for natural disasters and Kardashian cleavage, I saw an article on the increasing popularity of cloned cats. Not caring if this was a miracle from St. Gertrude of Nivelles or the result of Google's spying, I called the company from the article and learned that Ferd's body, stuck in my vet's freezer as collateral until I paid up, was a candidate for cloning. And one of the storage options actually cost (a lot) less than an iPhone. *Hallelujah!*

Feeling like a kid awakening to a large pile of brightly wrapped packages or an unattended pack of matches, I forwarded the instructions then breathlessly called my clinic to ask if they could pull his remains, biopsy them, and pop the samples off via FedEx overnight. Visions of another fat, fuzzy black kitten dancing in my head, I figured they would be excited for me. Napoleon also figured he could pull off a land invasion of Russia.

Because his cells were losing viability by the second, I had the sales rep dial the vet's office to explain the request coherently, something I suspected I was incapable of. Not long after, my phone rang. It was the clinic's manager, and she sounded like she was trying to describe the Spanish Inquisition to a classroom full of preschoolers. She kept repeating phrases like, "I'm trying to keep in mind that you're grieving" and "your dear, sweet boy." *What the fuck?*

Here I am thinking I just found the most sublime memorial possible for my cat, a chance for a kitty bearing his genetic code to spend another lifetime perfecting the arts of sloth, gluttony, and bloodthirstiness. Maybe I'd even let this one keep his testicles... Yet here was this person barely able to disguise the fact that my request was eliciting emotions akin to clubbing a harp seal pup with a rotting walrus cock while flossing with public toilet-seat pubes. And she was also telling me *no*.

Now never mind the fact that this person had never met my cat while he was still warm. Did *she* give him daily injections of IV drip fluids? Did *she* chase him around twice a day to shovel painkillers and chemo meds down his throat? Did *she* continually redo his menu so he wouldn't choke as lesions bloated his tongue? Did *she* spend nights deciphering pharmaceutical studies trying to find ways to keep him living and living without pain? Did *she* wrack her brain, sacrifice her own needs, and accost her friends and family to help pay for his treatment? Did *she* bathe the ubiquitous mess of canned food and trailing mucus off him, over and over and over? Did *she* agonize about when it would be time to humanely end his life? Was *her* left forearm now a solid mass of scars? *Fuck cancer.* But whatevs.

I swallowed my shock and tried to reason with her. My future cat's life depended on it. *Why couldn't they do it?* They didn't have time. *Could they slot me in if there was a cancelation?* No. *Why not?* Ferd died of cancer. *The type of cancer was highly localized and not genetic.* They'd have to defrost him. *Frozen samples are OK.* He's dead. *Don't they do necropsies when people ask for them?* It would be a health code violation to store the tissue in the refrigerator. *So where do you store your other biopsies?* We're busy. *What about tomorrow?* None of our staff feel comfortable performing this procedure. *Oh. Mmmm, OK. Really?*

I was beginning to get a whiff of a stench I hadn't gagged on in thirty years. The first time I was sixteen and working as a seasonal cashier at a farmer's market in Springfield, Illinois. I liked the people; I liked the job, and I thought I was pretty good at it. It was owned by a toothy, white-haired couple I could easily imagine offering warm apple pie and folksy yarns about local weather anomalies stretching back seven decades. They were so very *nice*. Up until it was time for seasonal layoffs, when I was told I, alone, wouldn't be asked back in the spring because I had been bringing tarot cards to work and giving other employees readings on our lunch breaks. *Oh*.

Never mind that the married, father-of-two manager was sleeping with a sixteen-year-old checker. Never mind that their favorite teen employee was a friend of mine who enjoyed shooting smack and getting into fistfights alongside his skinhead buddies in his spare time. Never mind that the other one was as dumb as a rock and hopelessly baked. Nope. It was me who got canned. For being a *witch*.

The second time was about a year later. I was working at a used record-and-anything-else-the-owner-could-hock store. My job was to sit there and look cute while the owner took naps or beer breaks in the basement and to listen to his big-fish stories while he was awake.

He was a local legend named Rick who never took off his mirrored aviator glasses. It was rumored that he didn't have eyes under those shades. I met him when I was twelve and the gang of middle-school delinquents I walked home with found out he would sell cigarettes to anything with lungs out of the illegal convenience store he was running from his living room. Also inhabiting the house were his mousy state-worker wife and two young children. Later, he branched out into reselling used cassettes that mostly came from smash-and-grabs. His business prospered, and he moved it across town. Eventually he could afford an ass in a seat, and I needed cigarette money.

Now, I was a damned good employee. I could chat up customers about music all day. When the rival bong shop next door filmed a TV spot with a giant-breasted woman bouncing around fingering the merchandise, my jailbait ass donned thigh-high boots, a half-shirt, and a tiny mini to lead a camera around our decidedly less impressive inventory. From then on in town, I was known as *The Rick's Girl*.

He liked me so much that he invited me and a couple of my friends to an election party in the shop basement. It was 1992, and there was Rick, his mistress, the night clerk, the Deadhead who sold used comics from the other half of the basement, and a handful of underaged punks getting drunk while the vote tallies came in. His girlfriend was a curvy creature. *I* was wasted on one can of cheap beer and started dancing around a pole in the basement with her, aiming to get a little closer. Then Rick stumbled over and stuck his tongue down my throat. *Ok, brush it off. No problem. Keep on rockin' in the free world.*

Since Rick knew my high school boyfriend from selling him cigs, he had probably assumed I was straight. At some point, he realized that I also had a girlfriend who came to visit me in the store. (Ok, maybe more than one.) It must have dawned on him that I was actually after his side piece in the basement that night, not him. A few months down the road after I had taken a night job slinging drinks at the local topless bar because *free titties*, this fine, upstanding gentleman pulled me aside and fired me because I was *gay* and might be a *bad influence* on his daughter. She was the same age I was when *he* started selling *me* cigarettes.

Back to the cat: it was sanctimoniousness I smelled through the phone. Comparable to week-old roadkill raccoon on an August afternoon, it's usually followed by the unharvested dingle-berry reek of hypocrisy. I was sure the people who were refusing to nick a piece off my dead cat weren't motivated by a clone taking a home from a stray kitten: I'd seen plenty of purebred animals prance through those doors. They'd been perfectly happy to offer him a biopsy while he was alive, and vets perform postmortem exams whenever they smell money in it. Hell, they had just stuck a needle in him the day before and stopped his heart. This was specifically about my intended use for the tissue. And it was glaringly obvious that the person on the phone thought that they knew what was better for my cat's corpse than I did. I could hear her voice grinding like a combine ploughing up my ear canal: *your dear, sweet boy…*

Cloning is, quite simply, creating an identical twin using the cells of another individual. Transgenic cloning is—literally—a whole 'nother animal (I'm still waiting for my eight-legged spider-chicken, Foster Farms!) The first cloned cat, Copy Cat, was born in 2001. She died at the ripe old age of 19. Her creator, Genetic Savings & Clone, charged around $50,000 to clone a cat. That's $78,722 in 2022 dollars. Now there are genebanks to choose from, and it costs $35,000 and falling fast. It's also increasing in frequency. However, for what I'm assuming is a large chunk of the population, cloning is a morally repellant concept. It used to belong to the realms of science fiction cautionary tales and fringe religious cults like the Raelians. Inexorably, cloning is moving into everyday life, Pietism be damned. *I'm* perfectly comfortable with xeroxed cats; I'm also the kind of asshole who would throw the switch from the Trolley Problem.

Now, I had run into anti-cloning sentiment before. Back when Yahoo News had a gloriously vicious comments section, I stuck my foot into the usual abortion screaming match by stating it was theoretically possible to undo an abortion by taking persistent fetal cells from a woman's tissues and putting them into denucleated eggs. Someone asked me to prove it, and I posted a research paper showing that those fetal cells live on, practically immortal, for the life of the host, rendering her a microchimera. My comment promptly disappeared—without explanation.

Not long after, a respected fertility clinic here in the US tried to run a study to see if it was feasible to use the same embryo splitting techniques that are used on cattle to produce identical twins in infertile women. This could allow women with only one viable embryo to have a larger family. The study was shut down, *also* without explanation.

Even natural identical twins freak a lot of people out. We like to think that we are all utterly unique and non-reproduceable. And well, we are—and we *aren't*. Just like identical twins aren't entirely alike, neither are clones. Due to epigenetic differences sparked by divergent environmental conditions, they are potential versions of the original donor that are bound to be very different beings by the time their lives run their course.

Some squeamishness about cloning has to do with a major misconception most people have about the nature of time and therefore their own existence. People tend to see themselves as discreet entities embedded in time and space, and time as something like a river that flows one direction. Einstein's theory of relativity posits space as two-dimensional support for 3D objects with mass, kind of like a fireman's jumping sheet, and time as the axis of the fourth dimension—illustrated using objects like the teseract that are best visualized by swallowing a massive dose of DMT. Neither is accurate as far as you or I are concerned. Lived time is a *material* phenomenon.

Imagine the universe flattened onto a single, vast sheet of graph paper. Now imagine it depicted as a torus (standard cake donut) on three axes. Zoom in down to the level of subatomic particles. Think of each of those particles as a point that is the result of a set of three-dimensional coordinates (a coordinate system). A nanosecond later, all the coordinates have shifted. Time is a sequence of each layered slice of paper flipping after the other like a kineograph (BTW, according to the second law of thermodynamics, the paper is *on fire*). Each is distinct from the next. There isn't *one* you in a lifetime. There are $2.52 \times 10^{18}$ yous in the average lifetime. It's the *sequence* binding them that makes each of us ourselves.

The set of coordinates that equals you and I changes entirely from nanosecond to nanosecond as the variable values adjust as a result of the movement of our atoms and molecules. In mathematical terms, this is known as (FUCK YEAH!) a *screw motion*. Our physical boundaries are so porous they might as well be imaginary, new material constantly bleeding into us via inhaled, ingested, and absorbed gasses, food, drink, drugs, chemicals, bacteria, viruses, and fungi and out of us via anus, urethra, vagina, testes, nose, mouth, sweat glands, pores, wounds, and shed hair and skin cells.

Even defined as starting at the epidermis, each of us is a subset of the entire set of numbers, a part of something else. We are, in any given instant, potentially reproducible–if the sums could be crunched and fed into a 3-D meat printer–and completely immortal in that the sequence that produced each of us can be expressed as a seizure-inducingly complex *formula* that can always run again, a concept introduced as *Laplace's Demon*, published by Pierre-Simon Laplace in 1814. The whole thing is probably hidden in *pi*, but that's another can of worms.

If you link a torus generated by one set of values to a mirrored image of itself, you get a Klein bottle, a *Möbius donut*. It also *loses* its orientability, the ability to determine a point in space using a left-right axis. Now attach a torus generated by a slightly different set of values to the first one at a point where they diverge. Then attach torii generated by all *possible* values together the same way, and you get a leviathan French cruller chock full of variants of you. This is the multiverse. Not sure if there is some sort of fruity filling. That's right, *God is fucking calculus*. And it turns out high school math is *actually useful*.

A being who was conjured from a set of these coordinates, mid ass-wipe, would lack the same quantum entanglements and relationship to the other points on the paper of the original, but they would start from the identical configuration of atoms they once held, with thoughts, feelings, and memories entirely reproduced. Now let's just take a moment to think about the implications this has for the concept of *free will*. The ego takes these facts like telling it its momma's a fat-ass-cock-eye-buck-tooth-no-chin-slack-jaw-hump-back-knock-knee-flea-bag-no-'count-trash-stankin'-clap-trap-crab-shack-roach-motel-cum-guzzlin-dumb-fuck ho who never loved it no-how.

Anyways, if I had known what I was walking into, I would have lied. I would have said I needed the samples taken for a study on the genetics of sublingual squamous cell carcinoma (by the way, I suggest you try that if you ever find yourself in my situation). Wrapped up in feel-good, unselfish motives, this pill would probably have slid right down the vet's throat, and I probably wouldn't be writing this.

Philosophical digression over and increasingly desperate, I began to beg. You see, it's much easier to produce cell lines from living tissue. If a pet is deceased, their cells remain alive and usable when refrigerated for up to five days. Some cells in the body can remain alive *weeks* after death. Frozen tissue, however, begins to lose viability immediately. By 24 hours in a freezer, chances of producing a live cell line are down to 50%. By two days, they are rapidly approaching zero. As the afternoon plodded on, I tried to use logic and eloquence, firing off an email. When the clinic closed for the night and no one had responded, I wrote again and let them know exactly how the situation was making me feel. *Pissed off.*

You see, one doesn't expect to be morally judged when paying for a service. When this happens after a gay couple tries to buy a wedding cake, the world takes notice. When a pharmacist turns down the money held by a woman standing in line for Plan B, there is an outcry. When a vet refuses to help a customer clone their dead cat? Well, my guess is I'd hear crickets.

But it's a similar situation: a denial of service because of an outrage to the provider's moral purity. Taboos around all three concern procreation and reproduction. Fucking for pleasure alone is non-pro-creative (for example, juicy same-sex romps or serving up a slice of cream pie after swallowing The Pill). Non-procreative sex is ubiq-uitously frowned upon in societies that are trying to beef-up their cannon fodder, bible-thumper, and wage slave populations, shore-up patriarchy, or control STDs. Cloning is the opposite phenomenon: procreation without sex. It limits genetic diversity, similarly to incest, another no-no. All are, to varying degrees, considered immoral by some segments of society, but not necessarily the *same* segments.

When I communicated these thoughts the next day, I was told I was free to come get my dead cat and get someone else to cut him up. And once I had my dead cat, never to darken their doorstep again. They backed that up by refusing to give my chronically ill *live* cat an extension on her lifesaving prescription until I could get her in with another clinic. *Touché.*

Unfortunately, my cat had had the bad taste to die four days before payday, and I was broke. The gene lab and my former vet were both letting me postpone payment a couple of days, but I highly doubted an unfamiliar clinic would, *if* I could even get an appointment any-where due to the pandemic pet population boom. Still, I called the lab to ask if it was possible to either send them the whole cat (no) or cryogenically preserve nonviable tissue until cloning science caught up (an emphatic *yes*). I dutifully began calling about looking for any-one with credentials willing to slice off a frozen chunk.

First, I tried the doctors recommended by the lab. All were booked solid for over a month. I called every reasonably close clinic, most of whom seemed interested in this potential new revenue stream, but there were still no open time slots. I was referred to humane societies, county dog pounds, specialist veterinary school labs, etcetera. No one could help me any time soon. Gradually, the horrific realization diffused in my head like a drop of blood in water: if I was going to do this, I was going to have to do it *myself.*

The next day was payday. The sun rose with me poring over the biopsy instructions the gene lab had sent to me to pass along to the clinic. At the grocery store, I bought ice packs, saline solution, and razors. At home, I tracked down a lab supply store where I could order online and pick up will-call. I scanned my receipt and, fearing I had botched it, called up, panicking.

I found myself on the phone with a helpful young man, stressing that I needed this stuff *NOW*. He repeated my list back to me:

Instrument Disinfectant - *check*.

Germicidal Wipes - *check*.

Gauze, Sterile 4" x 4" Tray of 10 - *check*.

Isopropyl Rubbing Alcohol 91% - *check*.

Dressing Forceps - *check*.

Latex Gloves, Sterile - *check*.

Surgical Scalpel, Single Use Sterile- *check*.

Vacutainer Conventional Blood Tubes, Red - *check*.

Urine Specimen Cup, Sterile - *check*.

Definitely not suspicious. When I inquired if the blood tubes would fit in the urine cup, he even tried them, and it was a no. And the tubes were a special order that wasn't in stock. *Shit.*

I still needed sterile tubes, a sterile container to put them in, and a Styrofoam shipping box to put all of it in. Off to Amazon I went, which guaranteed this was going to drag on into the next week since I couldn't ship the samples over the weekend. Sterile cryotubes and 50 ml centrifuge tubes purchased, I caught the bus. The store was located in a blighted industrial neighborhood, and I was Dante descending into Hell—but with Google maps guiding me instead of Virgil.

My first stop was at an Office Depot, looking for the Styrofoam box. Nope. They told me to go to FedEx. Back on the bus, I traveled deeper down MLK BLVD until it stopped on the Hawthorne bridge ramp. I found myself in a sprawling shantytown constructed from plywood and tin sheets.

All of the street signs were blurred. The further I walked, the worse my surroundings became. My phone was leading me down a desolate sidewalk behind a Goodwill Super Store. I stopped and slid my credit card into my bra. Under the Highway 99 overpass, there was a city of lean-tos. On my side of the street, I could see a man's foot protruding from the shadow of a building. A few feet further revealed a rusted RV with a young man laid out beside it and an orange, heavy-duty extension cord running across the street under the wheels of passing traffic.

I reached my destination and headed back, huffing and puffing, lugging a lab in a box. *Civilization!* At least I thought that's where I was—until I saw a man riding a bike the wrong way down the street wielding a homemade pike cobbled together from a machete blade and a steel fence post.

The FedEx store also didn't have the box, so I ordered it and boarded my bus home. The entire bus was packed with excitedly chattering intellectually disabled adults out on a day trip. An amorphous blob of uncanny dread in the center of my skull grew until it oozed, cold, out of my ears. I hopped off and made my way home, stuffing my underwear drawer full of sharp objects and flammable liquids upon arrival.

I had counted on working in peace for the procedure. My husband was *supposed* to be off for a weekend fishing trip, and my kids were *supposed* to be in school. When my children came running in the door to greet me, I learned to my horror that the younger two were going to be home for a teacher planning day. *Oh shit.* I was going to have to be a ghost in the walls.

The next day I felt faint and floaty. I waited. I waited for my oldest child to go to school. I waited for my husband to pack his van and head out of town. I waited for the Amazon delivery man. I re-read the instructions and sketched a 2 cm circle on a piece of scratch paper.

When it was safe, I arranged my purchases in the basement. Luckily, I had just bought a plastic sheet for a garden row cover. That went over an old army cot-*cum*-operating table. Then I noticed there was only one glove in the sterile packet. *Great.* Off to buy gloves and print the FedEx label.

Back home, I fought a funny, tight feeling in my chest, just like the afternoon Ferd died. I dropped off my gloves and called to remind the clinic that I needed to *borrow* my cat for a necropsy and would return him for cremation. They brought him out to me in a coffin-shaped cardboard box.

It was only a block walk back, but I live on one of the youngest, hippest, drunkest streets in Portland. I grimly headed down the road carrying a frozen cat, passing people eating and chatting and window shopping all around me. A hungry python wound around my ribcage.

Down the stairs we went, telling my kids I had work to do and not to disturb me. I should probably mention what I do for a living:

I make sculptures out of articulated skeletons taken from roadkill I find in the streets or rats my cats drag back to my yard. I handle dead things a lot. No one is surprised around my home to know I'm working on an opossum or raccoon in my basement studio. I had, however, never worked on a cat out of principle, particularly one I loved like a child. This was going to *suck*.

I laid out my tools, masked up, and started sterilizing. I opened the box. He was in a plastic bag, zip-tied shut with a tag on it. There was frost on his fur. Thankfully his eyes were closed. The snake stopped strangling me as I realized that Ferd *just wasn't there*. Wherever he was, it wasn't in this frozen corpse. This body was a liminal object, living in a past and a future but not in the *present*. I bit back bile.

The instructions stated that he should be shaved. Turns out that shaving a frozen cat is pretty hard to do. Fortunately, I had already asked the vet to shave off a large portion of his fur so I could have Victorian-style mourning jewelry made from it. I tried to shave the furless patch as close to the skin as possible. That part was passably easy. However, the lab wanted at least one ear-tip, and that was not going well: the ear bent and shifted away from the pressure of the blade.

I started disinfecting the prepped areas: iodine, then chlorhexane, then alcohol. The first sample was easy to take, physically. Just insert the scalpel and move it in a two cm circle. Two cms is surprisingly large on a body. It looks *painful*. My suspicions about taking samples from frozen flesh were, however, correct: the scalpel cut easier than it would have on thawed skin, and there was no blood to make a mess to add to the awfulness of the task. I opened a tube, inserted the sample, and filled it with sterile saline before capping it off, then scrawled his name and the date on it and dropped it into a centrifuge tube. Done. *Breathe.*

I took two more the same way. Next was the ear tip. 2 cms is basically the entire ear. This felt like mutilation. I knew that ear. I'd seen it swivel and flick so many times. I'd seen it aiming toward birds, cat food cans, and my voice making ridiculous kitty noises. I steadied myself, cut, and stuffed it into the tube. *Almost done.* As an afterthought, I decided to take his center back foot pad because that tissue is naturally tougher and might not have been as damaged by the freezing temperatures. A bit nauseated, I bagged the samples and put them in my work fridge to wait for Monday.

Alone with the remnants of my old friend, I took off my gloves and petted him for the last time, feeling his soft black fur without warmth or his purr rumbling under it. I packed him back up the way he had been given to me, washed my hands, and drifted out the door—to hand over my money and his body to be reduced to ashes, to be deposited into a small box, to be delivered back to me with a complimentary nose print.

But not all of his body. Some small pieces of him are Texas-bound—heading for temperatures so cold they cause flesh and bone to shatter like Christmas ornaments. There they will wait. Maybe forever. The storage fee is less than $10 a month, so I'm not losing much by hanging on to this dream. The lab even cut my bill by $150 when I told them what had happened, but I still had to borrow money from a friend (thanks, Ellie!) to pay Charon for all the crap I had to buy to enable my journey through the underworld.

But maybe, someday, cloning methods will improve enough to thaw out his kitty bits and coax them into living cells. A Japanese scientist has already cloned mice from bodies that had been conventionally frozen for sixteen years. And then maybe, just maybe, I'll get to sit back and heckle passing birds with a familiar-black cat crushing my lap to sleep.

nonfiction

# The First
## laura golden bellotti

We were only unequal in ways that didn't matter. I had a mother and you had a Jesus on the top bunk. When you were at my house, my mom treated you like another daughter. She considered your dad a friend and admired him for doing what no other dads did in those days. He handled the cooking, washed and ironed your clothes, signed your report cards, and was an enthusiastic audience during the plays we occasionally put on in your backyard for him and my mom: *Clues in the Barbeque Ashes*, *Mystery of the Golden Roller Skate*, and *Girls Who Sing Upside Down*. You not having your own mother? You never brought it up.

We didn't have to decide who was who. We were both. We switched back and forth without really thinking about it. One day you were Nancy Drew and I was George, her best friend. The next day I'd be Nancy and you'd be George—or Georgia, the weird name she was born with. We weren't mimicking anything from the book, we were acting out our own mystery. That was the thrill. Making up our own story as it unraveled, effortlessly falling into it and into our characters. Part them, part us.

It was always your backyard, not mine. Mine was bigger but flatter and too many flower beds. Yours was more fun. Craggy avocado tree, overgrown hill that sloped down from your small mint green house, rusty garden tools, clothesline with a drooping bag of clothes pins, and Trev, your aging black cocker spaniel who trailed behind us wherever the clues led. If you were the first to identify a clue, you'd announce in an eerie voice: *Nan-cy, cloo-ooze, white dog doo!* And I'd race over from the other end of the yard where I was also searching for suspicious objects. I'd slowly walk around the fossilized dog droppings, inspect them, kick them, and seriously consider what they could mean. *They've been here a long time, George, so the creature must be dead by now*, I'd say. *We'd better check behind those bushes.* We'd run over to the bushes that your father had warned us about, (*Don't eat the berries, they're poisonous.*) and if we didn't find anything there, we'd follow another mysterious sign. *These must be the footprints of the woman with no voice, who stares but never speaks,* you'd say. And I'd keep it going: *You're right! She was up to no good. And her high heels fit these prints. We must find her!*

Without a pause, you would take it from there. You'd point to the old lady hanging up her laundry next door and come up with reasons why she was most likely the villain. You'd whisper: *I've seen her bony, yellow fingers with pointy nails, and she gives me the evil eye when I'm riding my bike.* Then I'd turn to notice another obvious clue: a torn nightgown hanging from your clothesline. *That's hers! How did it get there, George? We have to investigate!*

When the sun was on its way down and your father called us in for dinner, we hadn't exhausted the mysteries. There were always more strange objects, unexplained coincidences, shady suspects.

I loved your dad's dinners. I liked that he brought us our plates already filled—with meat, potatoes, vegetables—rather than platters in the middle of the table like at my house. There were more people in my family than in yours, but I liked that at your house we were the unrivaled focus of your dad's attention. Just me and you. I loved his pork chops with gravy and buttery mashed potatoes. You made jokes about the apron he wore over his shirt and tie and about him being a good cook. He was an embarrassment for you because he was old enough to be your grandfather and because men weren't supposed to do the cooking. My father only cooked one thing: scrambled eggs on Sundays. But your dad did all the cooking all the time because he was the only parent in your house.

We talked only once about why you didn't have a mother. You had one, you told me after I'd asked, *but I never see her and it's okay,* you said. *Doesn't she want to see you?* I asked. You told me she had come around a few times to spy on you at our school playground. But you ignored her and never went over to the fence where she called to you. *She's just a crazy lady,* you said, like it was no big deal. I didn't ask you anything else. I could tell you were done talking about her. We were seven then, and you never mentioned her again.

Then there were the things you had that I didn't. But because I was at your house as often as at my own, I thought of those things as mine too. Like your redwood bunk beds. Taking turns sleeping on the top happened without us having to negotiate. As many nights as

I slept up there, the top bunk was always a thrill. Climbing the ladder, hitting my head on the ceiling, being above it all. And the small, framed picture of Jesus—blonde and serious—on the wall of the top bunk. He was another bunkmate. The bottom bunk was like sleeping in a cave. Dark and close. When I slept on the bottom, I loved to hear you singing to yourself at night or rolling over just above me, making the bed boards creak.

We never referred to the Jesus. Neither you or your father seemed religious, so I wasn't sure why he was up there anyway. Sometimes when you got mad—you'd accidentally drop a box of Cheerios and the O's flew across the floor, or Trev slobbered all over your new pedal pushers—you'd shout *Jesus H. Christ!*, pause to look over at your dad, and then you'd both burst out laughing. Still, the top bunk Jesus left an impression. No matter how many nights we stayed up laughing so loud that your dad had to knock on the wall to quiet us down, and as many times as we got away with stealing candy bars from the hallway cupboard and bringing the stolen goods back to our bunks, blonde Jesus remained solemn and calm.

We were still bunkmates in seventh grade when you started going for drives with Barry after school. This was long after our practice sessions touching tongues so we'd both be ready for boys. And it was a few years after we'd gotten our hearts broken when we saw Fabian, in the flesh, in a restaurant where my older sister was having her sweet sixteen party. He refused to give us an autograph and was crushingly unattractive anyway, nothing like his photos, which made us doubt the authentic lovability of celebrities. *Jesus H. Christ, what a loser,* you said. *How could anybody kiss him with all those pimples,* I said.

Barry was older than us, one of the cool guys from the high school we were still a few years from attending. We saw him at a coffee shop near our junior high, and all it took was just one look, as the song predicted. After grabbing the seat next to you at the counter, he asked if chocolate was your favorite flavor. When you nodded and gave him the look, he won you over with his ESP: *I could tell,* he said. He ordered chocolate shakes for both of us, paid the check, and that was it.

Your dad didn't know that several times a week Barry gave you rides after school and that you were making out with him at the beach. I was excited for you and glad to be the excuse for why you got home late. You explained to me how making out with Barry was different than when we touched tongues as young girls. *His tongue goes all the way inside your mouth,* you said, which sounded weird, *and then you do it back to him.* I asked you if it felt gross and you said he did it gently so you liked it. We weighed too much now for us both to sleep on the top bunk like we did sometimes when we were younger. But once in a while we'd sleep on the bottom together and we'd touch each other's developing breasts. *Does Barry do it like that,* I'd ask. *Much better than that,* you said, and we laughed too long and too loud until your dad started knocking on the wall.

Unlike my dad, who went to work in an office every day, your dad stayed at home. He was retired, you said, and got a check every month for the years he spent in the costume departments at movie studios. He'd tell us stories about all the old movie stars, most of whom we'd never heard of except for Doris Day and Marilyn Monroe. One actress had such big breasts, he said, that her bras had to be designed by her boyfriend who built airplanes. We didn't really believe that, but it was a funny story. And since we were in the throes of buying our first bras, we could relate. *Think Barry could design a good bra for you?* I asked. *Maybe he could make two—one for each of us. Actually,* you said, *he probably could—he draws cartoons, sexy ones, too.*

Barry was not only a good cartoonist; he was handsome and confident. We both admired his smooth skin and silky hair and slim body. He told you he was going to be in politics one day, which was why he was running for class president and had to give a speech in front of the whole high school. He practiced on you as he drove you home the day before the assembly. *Who knows,* you told me on the phone that night, *maybe I'll run for mayor of L.A. one day. I know I could make a good speech.* I knew, even then, that you were daring enough to do whatever sparked your imagination.

At thirteen, I wasn't exactly trailing behind you when it came to my attraction to boys, but my intensely felt crushes never amounted to anything tangible. As for making out, I had never made it past public kisses at spin the bottle parties. I had yet to be invited to take a ride to the beach alone with a high school boy. I don't think it was because you looked older. It was that you knew how to act older, which was why Barry wanted you and not me. Would I have gone with him if he had asked? Hearing your beach stories whispered to me on the bottom bunk, feeling both envious and relieved that it wasn't me French kissing an older boy, I still don't know how terrified or ecstatic I would have felt alone in the car with Barry. But it almost was me since it was happening to you.

Overhearing your end of one of our phone calls about Barry, your dad confronted you. He was more tolerant than my dad would have been, but he was upset that you had lied about where you were after school. He didn't forbid you from seeing Barry, but he wanted to meet him.

*That's not gonna happen,* you told me at one of our last sleepovers. *My dad is living in the dark ages.* I didn't understand why you didn't want your father to meet Barry, but of course I was on your side. *We'll figure it out,* I said. You looked at me with that look you would give your dad whenever you planned to defy him. *We?* you said.

Barry continued to come by our junior high after school. The two of you would talk for a few minutes, and then he'd drive away. Were you planning something? Meeting secretly somewhere? You never told me, and without discussing it we began a heartbreaking new routine: I no longer came to your house after school and you didn't come home with me. The sleepovers didn't happen anymore, and the phone calls tapered off. I missed you terribly but imagined you off in some hidden place with Barry and was rooting for you. One day at lunch I asked if you'd figured out a way to see him. *Don't worry, I won't ask you to lie for me anymore,* you said. You didn't sound like yourself. *I'm not worried,* I said. I was talking to someone who looked like you, but you were gone.

We moved on, as people now say. You had many boyfriends; I had a few. You sang your own songs at our high school talent show. I worked on the school paper. I went to college. You travelled to India and Nepal. We kept in touch every so often but rarely saw each other.

Because of what your son has asked of me, I've been thrown back to our girlhood searching for clues to unresolved questions: who made the first move when we were seven? what drew us to each other? why was our friendship as exhilarating as a romance, but so much easier? what was it about us together that made me crave spending every free moment with you?

I always assumed that what made us inseparable was how alike we were. But that's not really the way it was. You shouted *Jesus H. Christ!* I felt reverent on the top bunk, even though I'm Jewish. You laughed when you rammed into a garbage can on roller skates and broke your arm. I was secretly scared of the trampoline but faked it every day in the summer before fifth grade so you could do your wild jumps. It was my idea to write *Girls Who Sing Upside Down.* It was your idea to touch tongues.

We loved the other in each other. We loved each other without calling it love.

Was the break-up just part of our mysterious chemistry? Girl meets girl, they submerge in friendship too deep to untangle—until the untangling, without a way to weave themselves back together.

In my early twenties, I visited your dad to get some advice about a job I was considering in the film business. He was a very old man by then. *You're better than that,* he told me. *Don't get involved in the movie business. It's not a nice business.* Your father had always spoken so fondly of his time in Hollywood making costumes for everyone from Rudolph Valentino to Jane Russell. When we were kids, you and I would jokingly ask him to call that director friend of his and have him put the two of us in a movie together. *Why not?* he'd say with a smile, but of course we were just kidding around. The movie business was his line of work, not something we wanted for ourselves.

I asked him what he meant by his anti-Hollywood remark. He told me that your mother had been an unknown movie actress and that the company she kept had been her undoing. He got custody, promising himself when you were a baby that he would keep you from her. *She never pulled herself out of the mess she made,* he said, and *I didn't want my daughter under her influence.*

You must have been told a version of your family history before we met. And your dad likely filled you in as you got older. It makes sense that you wouldn't have wanted to talk about it when we were young. And as we grew up, I guess we had more important things to think about than your mother.

I ended up taking the film job but worked only briefly in the not-nice business before developing other interests.

When you returned from the first of your many overseas travel adventures, my mom heard you were getting married and offered to throw you a bridal shower. You told her you weren't really into showers, but because it was her, you gratefully accepted. *I think of her as Mom,* you told me when we saw each other at the shower. You'd never actually said so, but it made sense. My mother adored you, and without putting words to it, you had adored her, too. At the shower, you told me that one of your most treasured memories was of being at our house on Mother's Day and bringing my mom breakfast in bed. I had no memory of it. It would have been just one more Mother's Day for me.

When your son called yesterday, I wasn't prepared. You and I had not been in contact much beyond birthday cards, neither of us ever forgetting the other's *day of earthly arrival,* as we aptly called it on your tenth birthday. We had met for dinner a few times over the last thirty years, but we were in our own spheres. As I followed your online postings, you inspired me with your wild journeys to every continent on Earth. There was beautiful you in Tanzania hiking to some treacherous peak; frozen California girl reveling and ice fishing in Greenland; righteously boozing it up with Irish comrades; dancing to the magic of the Aurora Borealis.

You traveled alone, leaving your less daring husband behind, falling in with fellow adventure-hustlers along the way. With summers off from your job, you didn't mind spending your modest income on getting you wherever you wanted to go. As soon as you returned from one far-flung jaunt you began planning the next one. I was never jealous. Comparing my humble exploits to yours was never the point. What thrilled you thrilled me.

The part of me that was us is still there. Although we weren't close as adults, spoke and socialized infrequently, it didn't matter. Because at seven, eight, nine, and ten through thirteen? We were as intimate as two humans could ever be. And that earliest bond doesn't break.

So, when your son asked me to visit you sooner rather than later, I rushed to you. You wanted me to be the last to see you. And while I was initially stunned by your request, it made sense. Of the many connections you had forged over a lifetime, ours needed to be the last. Because it was a clue. Because it was easy and true. Because it was the first.

# Body: A Definition

### wendy m. thompson

*Body: referring or pertaining to the entire physical structure of a human or animal including bones, flesh, and organs.*

As a child, I was taught that we could not own our own bodies. In a house where a father the size of forest fire burned through every room, every wall, every layer of soft tissue and pink fleshy membrane, all the power belonged to him. And our bodies, the old growth, had no chance against his mouth of destruction, flames charging through our underbrush. It was a reminder and fact that in that house, there was no way to prevent a forest fire. We grew so tangled and tired of our own fear, our limbs holding onto each other for the millionth time as the blaze sucked out all the air, that we gave in to the incineration.

My father's rage would jump highways to steal our privacy, forcing us to dress in open door bedrooms and insisting that we perform 90-degree angles of gratitude and mechanical armed gestures of jubilation under the threat of deforestation. There was no holiday or public space that he did not control. What was a body when it belonged in someone else's national forest?

And yet, I was a stubborn tree. One that grew crooked intentionally. One that ruined the postcard image he tried so hard to craft for the outside world. One that visitors and strangers came around after hours and in the middle of the night, jumping fences, wanting to see. I would find ways to steal my power back when and where I could. Hiding in a closet with a razor blade, each drop of red a breadcrumb for whoever might come looking. Turning away ever so slightly in family pictures to disappear myself from view. These were the small ways that I knew my body still belonged to me: when I secretly spoke the words I really wanted to say under my tongue, only to say them out loud when I became older, inviting a terrifying inferno of violence to erupt from his body.

I was scorched earth, then, but I was free. New growth under the ash of old branches and trunk that he could not easily reignite or smother.

*Body: referring to fullness, volume, or a substantial quality of flavor.*

We were not supposed to want ourselves. We were raised to resent the biological ways our bodies grew: the thick protrusion of brown thighs and hips, the brown equatorial mark of our skin. That skin. A brown external layer of epidermis that unnerved a maternal aunt who forecast the eventual spoliation of her half black nieces under the magnificent sun, its warm rays striping us brown like tigers. If we did not stay out from under it, if we did not stay indoors away from it, we would surely contribute to the black ruin of our taupe futures and tan phenotype. Of all my mother's children, I was the one who looked the least like her. Of all my mother's children, I knew from birth what it meant to be dark before darkness was given a name, before I gave birth to my own beautiful and loving darkness: a daughter and a son.

*Body:* 身体 *(Shēntǐ)*

What did I carry in my body?

That I was raised by a Chinese immigrant mother. That I attended a school where nearly all the kids were white. That my few black peers would accuse me of thinking I was so cute and talking so white and having such good hair that my mother would angrily yank a comb through every morning. All of these strands would leave me feeling strange about being black in my own body and I would relate to it in pieces or scenes: an arm then goosebumps, a sudden sound, an eyelash swept into the wet white surface of the sclera, a taste of something bitter, something sweet, a snide remark over dinner, a cold sore in the mouth, a stifled sob in public, a bruise on the leg, a trifling unforgivable gesture, a clavicle, a body that is an island under speculation by developers and inhabited by hostile natives, a psoriatic plaque spilled like cranberry juice staining the brown beach of my lower back, an infestation of ants after someone forgot to close the jar, a rupture, recession, a short rib with no meat on a hungry plate, a stab wound to the heart (metaphorically), an unshaved leg rubbed against a demanding erection.

I would gravitate toward reading in order to survive: reading the room, reading a book to escape, pretending to read a poster or an old medical bill or a scrap of paper I dug out of the bottom of my cavernous purse whenever I was in a public place and felt utterly alone and terrified.

My insides: a worn book that had been read over and over, its pages dull and creased, its spine cracked.

My insides: an unread book that had yet to be touched after being bought with the intent of being read on a ten-hour flight.

I would face the world and run from problems in this body: short, loud, hairy, greasy, myopic, big foreheaded, thick in small places, flat where it should have been curved, bony, bent, brown, ashy, musty, wet, two-toned. I would feel ashamed in this skin while fighting customer service agents with this body. Would stand too long in too many dressing room mirrors or hiding under sheets in front of new lovers with this body. But where I felt protected, what made me know I was well insulated and ready for every possible confrontation, was the shine. In lieu of magical amulets or a cultural inheritance of abundant epidermis, I had the protection of grease, layers applied directly out of the family value size jar of Vaseline to the body from childhood. And where my two sisters would find the soft side of a loofa drenched in lavender and oat milk, I would submerge myself in it: the slippery, the glistening, the oily. Grease for grits and Blue Magic for scalp and petroleum jelly for slick lips. Grease like fatbergs stuffed in the throats of subterranean sewer pipes. Grease like it took all night for Howlin Wolf to make that final cut of "Smokestack Lightning."

If there was an opposite of clean and crisp and beautiful and dainty, I would drown in it. Willingly.

But there is always a price to pay with whatever you choose to do with your body. My mother taught me that. And there would be no day that she would rest from reminding me:

*No decent Chinese girl would ever carry herself in her body like that.*
*No decent Chinese girl should enjoy those parts of her body that much.*

*Body: a large or substantial amount of something; a mass or collection of something*

When I became an adolescent, I was told that despite my blackness and my femaleness depreciating the social and economic value of my body, it was still worth something. Both my parents would make this clear to me in their own way, that my body, however non-white and non-male, should not under any circumstance be given away for free. Specifically, I was told never to offer my body to any man regardless of what he might promise to give me in return.

But growing up in a house where the distribution of endearments was thin and the gifting of abusive, defeating words was plentiful, I wanted nothing more than to receive a lifetime of validation: to be fully seen, to be heartily fed, to be eagerly touched. And being that my house existed in a patriarchal nation where consent had always been at the discretion of boys and men and men were always given access, and women were expected to wait to be chosen, I would listen to predators, not my parents, who taught me that my body not only operated as a form of currency but that I could barter it for things I so desired.

Over the course of my lifetime, the asks were always small and the payment on my end always steep: a paid-for dinner at an expensive restaurant–my entire body, an hour of a man's time to come and replace my garage sensor light or cut back an overgrown oleander in my backyard–my entire body, the chance to feel human at the hands of another, however forceful or abusive. Always, always, the payment of my entire body.

*Body: as in, "Damn, she got a nice…"; as in "All he wants is my…"*

Despite having men eat at the good corners and steal from my body, despite them picking through and discarding the flesh and excess organs they felt did not serve them, my body would travel across continents and oceans to find joy in another body far from home.

I would land a postdoctoral fellowship at a Midwestern public research university where I should have remained focused on my immediate priorities: applying for tenure track academic jobs at elite universities, writing, revising, submitting manuscripts for publication, and teaching courses for the history department. But I was confident that my American passport and the few words my mother taught me as a little girl would be enough to last me two weeks in China where I went to conduct field research in Guangzhou, a city that had become home to a large Nigerian urban trading community that made the news following a protest by Nigerian nationals in response to a fellow countryman jumping out of a second story window to evade a passport check during an immigration raid.

This was research, not a love affair. This was a marriage for citizenship, not a romance. This was a misunderstanding, not a means for building a future. I was a rising scholar from California who was working on a project that wove together Chinese immigrant and black life in the New World. He was from Lagos and had previously worked as a machine operator at a Lebanese-owned biscuit factory, a security guard, and an assistant at his father's printing press before taking his chances as a petty trader in Asia.

For me, China was where everything we used and wore and broke and discarded came from. For him, China was the pocket and the capital and the hand that filled it. To know it through him, China was the beginning of the world.

Between our bodies, we would create a family, moving from coldest place to coldest place: a village in New York's Adirondack foothills, a gateway town to Maine's mid coast, a city in western Indiana, a small white middle class, once Jewish corner in the older working-class half of the Twin Cities. Living semi-temporarily in apartments and rented spaces that were never home to us, these were the years that we dreamed of a house big enough to hold us and all the things we loved: art, music, books, plants, our daughter's overproduction of collages and illustrated stories, long distance phone calls to Nigeria, a dark place to store all of the trauma. These were also the years that we recognized the limits of our bodies, the fragility of limbs and digestive systems, the weight of small children felt in the spine, the sadness of one's own degrading eyesight while sitting with a squinty six-year-old during her first eye exam.

What did it mean to enter and exit a country in a body with first world privilege? To be a woman whose mobility was defined by her citizenship? To enter into the worlds of others with American research money? To meet a man who moved undocumented through a foreign city in a body marked illegal due to a lack of valid visa status? To begin to know and love the widest part of blackness? To watch others ontologically read his Africanness as primitive and his immigrantness as infantile? To represent a pathway to the American Dream for someone who once dreamed of seeing London and New York as a boy in Lagos? To relive my father's relationship to my immigrant mother; his hand holding all the money, all the decision-making power? To be unafraid of the worries of the female relatives on your father's side who were convinced he was using me for papers? To believe others when they say that they love you? To believe that you are worth loving?

Nothing could have prepared me for marrying a predator.

*Body: the main or central part of something, especially a building or a text.*

When I became a mother, I watched my children closely, curious as to how they would turn out. Their complexions brown like mine. Their skin and hair, warm and fibrous like each stick and feather woven through a bird's nest. Their small bodies smelled like metallic new birth held together by bones, strong like freshly crafted earthen pots. They were vessels into which I poured half of my own genetic material, all of my immunities and disorders: allergies, rashes, hairlines, tooth symmetry. And those not tied to physiology: food pickiness, frugality, a tendency toward timidity and bookishness. Their other half would come from their father which is why my son was born with a tiny dangling sixth finger on both of his hands and why my children would sprout tall and strong, towering over me and shedding blankets of needles like redwoods all before the age of 12.

When I was first pregnant with my daughter, I could feel the swell of my father's disappointment in having a girl repeated in the bow of my own uterus, in my feet and against my bladder. For nine months, I had wanted a son.

Before she even came out of my body, everyone kept asking, "Do you think you'll have another?" And then my daughter came and I found myself relearning all of the final, explicit, and indirect ways a black girl in this world can be ruined. Childrearing, after all, is a cumulative process and requires experiential learning, however structurally violent and interpersonally terrifying. It was key to learning how to be a more protective and defensive mother. How else could a woman running perpetually from her problems care for her child in a room full of other mothers built like campsite bears? How else could a person susceptible to choosing verbally abusive partners be trusted enough to parent her children who withdrew into shells of their own silent making?

Instead, whenever the opportunity for confrontation and rage presented itself, I would always succumb to the feeling of wanting to claw my way into a wall. Like the time at the children's museum when a white woman, trying to take a picture of her own son, grabbed my daughter's wrist and yanked her out of the way. Or the time when a group of black children who received free school lunches called my daughter poor for wearing the same jacket to camp every day and told her she was lying when she said she had two thousand dollars in her savings account. Or the time when a triangle of white girls, who had never owned a passport, denied that Disneyland Paris was a real place as they accused my daughter of lying about traveling to France.

In these moments, I wanted nothing other than to become an absolute unnamable fucking monster, to gut and skin all the bears in the camp and knock down all the walls. In these moments, I wanted nothing more than to be a mother holding my child close to my chest, away from dark water, jagged rock, quicksand.

When I was pregnant with my son, I was terrified by the reality that I would be giving birth to a boy. A black boy with a big head and brown eyes who would grow into a young man able to count birthdays and police encounters in which he would be profiled and accosted by officers who wouldn't give a damn about the meaning of his name. A boy whose right to life—that bird chest, those lovely mom kisses—would be unacknowledged as he lay pressed into the dead of pavement in the dead of night. A trespasser. A Trayvon. A boy born into a legacy of black men who all tell the same story of the first time they were perceived as a threat: a white woman, her purse, the clutch in an elevator, the deliberate decision to cross the street, the driver and passenger inside a parked car, their fearful glances, the sound of the locking mechanism clicked twice for surety. There is always a mix of pain, bewilderment, resentment, and ridicule that is audible in their voices when they tell the story. I never tell them that I can hear it. The sound of a human full of beauty and compassion and potential and trauma being made into an absolute unnamable fucking monster.

I had them in this order: girl, boy.

I only hope in my lifetime they will forgive me for everything harmful that I gave them, that they did not want or need, and everything useful that I could not afford them.

*Body: verb. To murder someone (black English)*

Penal Code 288.5 - Any person who either resides in the same home with the minor child or has recurring access to the child, who over a period of time, not less than three months in duration, engages in three or more acts of _____ with a child under the age of 14 years at the time of the commission of the offense is guilty of the offense of _____.

And then, one day, he would invade and violate the body of my _____: men funneling out of a wooden horse to storm the gates of the girl when I wasn't home.

He would put the boy in front of the TV and turn the back bedroom into a crime scene.

My _____ would cease to have a body.

My _____ and I would be left to carry this felony, a betrayal too horrific to say. For which I would have given the last page of life, the book of my own body, to reverse, to undo.

*Body: organ, office, mechanism, stratagem, intrigue*

Why would I not become an island given all I had lived through? Deserted. Inaccessible. Full of wild things. Placed in the furthest fantastic region of an ocean body. Overgrown with fragments of an unhindered imagination and yellow lupine. Why would I not intentionally try to disappear given how I'd been built? A house made of bones and teeth, hands pulling at fresh stitches. The hard leather falling open to reveal the small pitted fruit of a still beating heart. Why would I not let my killers come to prey on me at my most vulnerable hour, professing fake love while in their pockets were knives, no condiments, and a moist towelette to wipe off the blood?

They would come to me to do what killers do: consume, cut, eviscerate, deny, demolish, lick the dinner plate, retch, violate, masticate, flee, dissolve. And it would take decades to relearn this body: bandaged, bent, splinted, starved, soft bellied, betrayed, scarred, fully loaded with extra cheese, rolled in heartbreak and sprinkled with too much man chasing, face to the wind, open hearted, smeared with wanderlust, shit, mud, and salt, a divine being on vogues, three stars forming a constellation, an old house with good bones, loose skin like a parachute that's kept me from falling from 9,000 feet twice, a thing to be loved and loved on, an entire ass erogenous zone (sex drive on toast), *aha!*

Now at 41, I use other words to describe my body: a soft thunder and the halo of lightning lining the horizon, a prayer amended, an apology without the "but," a return after Katrina, a story revisited and revised after twenty years, an earthenware clay pot filled with cooked rice, a Negro spiritual cloaked in two Chinese operas, the art of making art that blooms from the chest, something broken made into mosaic, something torn turned into collage, a psoriatic blemish on the skin's sky that is an epidermal borealis, once the hammer now the axe, once the captain now the judge, once the ship now the kite.

I am a verb. *To surrender.* I am an action. *To love.*

To surrender to love in this body.

# Issue 12 Contributors

Laura Golden Bellotti is a nonfiction author, short story writer, and ghostwriter living in Los Angeles. Her short stories have appeared in anthologies, literary journals, and other print media, including *West*, the *Los Angeles Times* Sunday magazine. Ms. Bellotti was the developmental editor of the best-selling *Women Who Love Too Much* and has since collaborated on numerous nonfiction titles. Books she has co-authored include *Parents Who Cheat*, *Latina Power*, and *You Can't Hurry Love*.

Toni La Ree Bennett's verbal and visual work has appeared in *Cimarron Review*, *Caesura*, *Gold Man Review*, *Cirque*, *Gravel*, *Puerto del Sol*, *Hawaii Pacific Review*, *december*, and *Memoir* with a poetry chapbook publication by Finishing Line Press, *Solar Subjugation*, among other publications. She lives with a feisty finch named Puppette. Photography and writing samples can be seen at www.tonibennett.com.

William Hawkins has been published in *Granta*, *TriQuarterly*, and *ZYZZYVA*. He currently lives in Los Angeles where he is at work on a novel.

Raul Herrera Jr. is a playwright, educator, and spoken word artist who has been involved with the Los Angeles-based education nonprofit, Get Lit - Words Ignite, for over 10 years. His writing is featured in *Get Lit Rising*, *Coiled Serpent* published by Tia Chucha Press and, in 2017, he wrote *Dante*, a modern Hip-Hop adaptation of Dante's Inferno, produced by Tim Robbins and The Actor's Gang Theatre. He plans to continue his pursuits in screenwriting and education.

Judd Hess holds a BA from the University of California, Irvine and both an MFA and an MA from Chapman University. He has won the Fugue Poetry Prize, the John Fowles Creative Writing Prize for Poetry, the Ellipsis Prize, and been nominated for the Pushcart Prize. His work most recently has appeared in *Philadelphia Stories*, *Temenos*,

*Making Waves: A West Michigan Review, Connecticut River Review, Gold Man Review*, and *Untenured*.

R. M. Janoe is a U.S. Navy veteran, writer, and homeschooling dad with an MFA in Creative Writing from National University. His work has been published in *Flash Fiction Magazine*. He lives on an island in the Salish Sea with his wife and daughter.

M. Kolbet teaches and writes in Oregon Recent work includes poetry in *Revolute, Scapegoat Review*, as well as fiction in *Imitation Fruit.*

Barb Lachenbruch's writing is inspired by her years of questionable work/life balance as a professor of forest biology and mother, wife, and daughter. Nowadays, she splits time between Corvallis, Oregon, where she substitute teaches, and her Coast Range cabin. Her work has appeared in *High Country News, CALYX: A Journal of Art and Literature by Women*, and *Stories (Within): An Anthology of Stories Within Stories*. She can be reached at barblachenbruch.com.

Priscilla Long's most recent book is on thriving while aging while creating: *Dancing with the Muse in Old Age* (Coffeetown, 2022). Her two poetry books are *Holy Magic* (MoonPath Press) and *Crossing Over: Poems* (University of New Mexico Press). Her how-to-write book is *The Writer's Portable Mentor: A Guide to Art, Craft, and the Writer's Life*. She grew up on a dairy farm on the Eastern Shore of Maryland. For more info go to www.priscillalong.com.

Daniel O'Leary is a recent MFA graduate from the Creative Writing program at Antioch University, Los Angeles. He lives and writes in Santa Cruz, CA and spends an unsustainable amount of time penning and sending nonsensical postcards which can be found at SixInchNonsense.com.

Michael Pearce's poems and stories have appeared in *The Gettysburg Review, The Threepenny Review, The Sun, The Yale Review, Conjunctions*, and elsewhere, and have won several national prizes (New Ohio Review, Oberon, The Tennessee Williams Prize in Fiction, and others). His collection of poems, *Santa Lucia by Starlight*, won the Brighthorse Prize in Poetry and will be published this year. He lives in Oakland, California, and plays saxophone in the Bay Area band Highwater Blues.

Eileen Pettycrew's poems have appeared or are forthcoming in *New Ohio Review, CALYX, The Normal School, Gold Man Review, Prime Number Magazine, Peregrine Journal, The Westchester Review*, and *SWWIM Every Day*, among others. She lives in Portland, Oregon.

Timothy Reilly had been a professional tubist (including a stint with the Teatro Regio of Turin, Italy) until around 1980, when a condition called "Embouchure Dystonia" put an end to his music career. Twice nominated for a Pushcart Prize, he has published in *Zone 3, Fictive Dream, Superstition Review, The Main Street Rag*, and many other journals. He lives in Southern California with his wife, Jo-Anne Cappeluti: a poet and scholar.

Joel Savishinsky is a retired anthropologist and gerontologist. His *Breaking the Watch: The Meanings of Retirement in America*, won the Gerontological Society's book prize. Poetry, fiction and essays of his have appeared in *Atlanta Review, Beyond Words, Caesura, The New York Times, SLANT*, and *Windfall*. His collection *Our Aching Bones, Our Breaking Hearts: Poems on Aging* will appear in 2023. He lives in Seattle, and considers himself a recovering academic and unapologetic activist. savishin@gmail.com

Layla Schubert occupies herself making sculptures from dead things and selling them to weirdos in Portland, Oregon. Her written work has been published in *Diverse Voices Quarterly, Heart Journal*, and the anthology, *Veils, Halos, and Shackles*. She also wrote a PhD dissertation that has probably been read by a total of five people. And she is a bit obsessive about her cats.

Claire Scott is an award winning poet who has received multiple Pushcart Prize nominations. Her work has appeared in the *Atlanta Review, Bellevue Literary Review, New Ohio Review, Enizagam*, and *The Healing Muse* among others. Claire is the author of *Waiting to be Called and Until I Couldn't*. She is the co-author of Unfolding in Light: A Sisters' Journey in Photography and Poetry.

Katya Suvorova is currently working on a memoir about her childhood experiences as an undocumented Russian immigrant. Her essays 'I Never Stopped Learning English for You,' and 'How 90 Day Fiancé Helped Me Tell My Story as the Child of a Mail Order Bride' are published in *JMWW journal* and *Memoir Magazine*. She is represented by Natalie Lakosil at Irene Goodman Literary Agency. You can find her on Instagram and Twitter: @suvorovawrites

Wendy M. Thompson is an Assistant Professor of African American Studies at San José State University. Her creative work has most recently appeared in *Roanoke Review*, *The Ana*, *Rigorous*, and is forthcoming in a number of other publications. She is the coeditor of *Sparked: George Floyd, Racism, and the Progressive Illusion*.

R. Thursday (they/them) is a writer, educator, historian, and all-around nerd. When not subverting Middle School Social Studies curriculum, they can be found reading, cooking spicy dishes, playing video games, watching cartoons, or writing about vampires, superheroes, queerness, mental health, space, tardigrades, on and on very good days, all of the above. They've been published by some pretty nifty places, and live in South King County, Washington, with the world's most copacetic cat.

Ashwin Vaidyanathan grew up in the Bay Area, but now teaches computer science as a visiting professor at Morehouse College in Atlanta. Outside of work, he enjoys playing team sports, reading, and racing his sister in Mario Kart Wii, even though she usually wins. "Forever Racing" is Ashwin's first short story publication.

Kory Vance is a poet, fiction writer, affordable housing professional, and strength athlete. In his poems, Kory uses experiences from an eclectic life to create alternative worlds that shine a light on our own. His work can be found in *The Antonym*, *The Salmon Creek Journal*, *HASH Journal*, the *SoFloPoJo*, and more. He is currently working on his first full volume of poetry, titled *Bury me with Rosemary*. Follow Kory's work on Instagram @strength_and_poetry.

Ash Witherell is a box in the attic. Their work has been featured in *Angel Rust Magazine*, and they're the author of a chapbook entitled "Urban Mythologies." They are slowly growing wings.

notes

www.ingramcontent.com/pod-product-compliance
Lightning Source LLC
Chambersburg PA
CBHW021932170626
46807CB00007B/3077